This book is dedicated to my daughter Laney. The spark, the heartbeat, and the reason this story exists.
It was your idea first, and I just tried to keep up.

Love, Dad

INTRODUCTION

Okay, before I throw you into the chaos, let me give you the *speed run* on meeting the Martins so you don't drown in names:

• Jimmy Martin (Dad): The nerd king of sci-fi and fantasy. If Gandalf had a YouTube channel, it would look just like his. Sure, he can be embarrassing at times, quoting lines as if he's auditioning for Comic-Con, but he's also the one who taught me to love stories and find magic in the ordinary. He drives me crazy and makes me proud all at once.

• Ashley Martin (Mom): The ultimate mama bear. She's protective, sharp, and can see through anything. If something feels off, she's already five steps ahead. She's my closest confidante. We share laughs, have long talks, and truly understand each other. However, she can switch into protect mode in an instant, and when that happens, you don't question her instincts. You simply follow her lead.

• Kali Martin (24): She embodies calm, big-sister energy. A *TikTok* influencer, she also serves as the family coach. Kali is the one who calls the plays, maintains harmony, and manages to make everyone feel like they're on the same team. When chaos arises, she is the voice that cuts through the chaos. In fact, she's the first person I turn to when I need advice that I'm willing to accept.

• Destiny Martin (24): Lives out of state and teaches middle school. She is soft-spoken, caring, and a professional worrier. Destiny feels everything more deeply than the rest of us, always checking in and wanting to ensure that nobody is left behind. If Kali is the coach, then Destiny is the heart—gentle and thoughtful, the kind of sister who can calm you down just by saying your name.

• Bryce Martin (22): A college gamer and esports captain, Bryce is a genuinely nice guy with a touch of anxiety. He's the kind of brother who truly cares, even when he's feeling overwhelmed by the demands of classes, gaming, and everyday life. Although he worries more than he lets on, he's always there for me when I need support. Quiet and steady—that's Bryce.

• Dylan Martin (17): Brash and athletic, he's always on the move. He'll leap into a fight without even asking what it's about—especially if it means protecting one of us. Stubborn and loud, he can be difficult to deal with at times, but beneath that tough exterior lies a heart of gold. He embodies big-brother energy, whether you want it or not.

• Grady Martin (13): My baby brother. He has a soft heart and is sensitive, giving hugs like it's his job. He worries about everyone, but when it truly matters, he shows bravery beyond his years. Quiet and thoughtful, he's the one who notices the things the rest of us miss.

• Grandma is old-school and firmly believes that robots should have remained in the movies. Half the time, she cracks one-liners that make us choke on our food; the other half, she reminds us that she has lived through worse. She's tough as nails, with a side of sass.

• Will Garcia is Kali's fiancé and feels like family already. He is kind, respectful, and shares Destiny's anxiousness, yet remains steady in all the ways that matter. You can count on him for anything, whether it's for a ride, a favor, or simply showing up when you need him the most.

• And then there's Dexi, who is 100% Mom's dog, and Izzy, who is most definitely my dog, our poodles. One's a guard dog in a perm, the other thinks she's a deer.

Got all that? Good.

CHAPTER 1
WELCOME TO MY TOTALLY NORMAL LIFE (NOT REALLY)

IF YOU'RE READING this because you want to know how my *very average* sixteen-year-old life turned into a front-row seat to the robot apocalypse, hi. I'm Laney. I'm 5'4" on a good hair day, athletic enough to still tie my shoes after gym class, with brown hair, blue-green eyes, and a recently licensed menace behind the wheel of a Jeep I love like a first pet. I'm funny *(confirmed by at least three humans and one guidance counselor)*, and I care way too much about people to be truly cool. Especially my brother Grady, who is thirteen and basically a walking hug with legs.

I live in Willow Springs, population forty thousand, where autumn is a postcard and the HOA has opinions about your Halloween skeletons. We live in one of those "AI Towns" you may have seen on the news, where traffic lights operate autonomously, your front door alerts you if you forget to lock it, and every restaurant is testing a chrome-elbowed waiter named "G.R.E.G". It's October, which means this place is pumpkin spice and football by day and drone shadows and LED jack-o'-lanterns by night.

If you think that sounds cozy and futuristic in a cute way, congratulations, you are my dad.

If you think that sounds like the opening scene of a safety video where a smart fridge eats a toddler, congratulations, you are my mom.

And if you think both of those things and would still drive your Jeep with the windows down just to feel something human, welcome. You might be me.

Anyway, I didn't wake up and decide, "Let's narrate my downfall to the internet." I honestly thought I was going to have a normal junior year: pass chemistry, avoid cafeteria food, drive my Jeep, keep Grady out of his feelings, and maybe, just maybe, I would figure out what it is I want to do after I graduate.

But then the future knocked. Loudly.

Keystone Cybernetics, the government-sanctioned tech giant responsible for many of our new technologies, decided to put their CEO on every screen in America to announce a *"new era of home assistance."*

Translation: humanoid robots for families. Affordable(ish), integrated with town systems, safety-first—all those buzzwords that make investors clap and Ashley (my mom) reach for the off switch.

Jimmy (my dad) muted the announcement just long

enough to say, "Okay, everyone, tell me that didn't look really cool."

My mom folded her arms. "Tell me you didn't just say that out loud."

I was sprawled on the rug, pretending not to listen while texting my best friend Mia.

If my parents buy a murder bot with Wi-Fi, I'm moving into your garage.

She sent back sixteen skull emojis and a photo of her cat wearing devil horns. Classic Mia.

Dexi, my mom's dog, except when she makes a mess, then she's the family's dog, our ten-year-old poodle, gave a sharp bark from the doorway, like she agreed with Mom.

Dexi barks at leaves, Amazon drivers, and occasionally clouds, but I swear this one was perfectly timed for *"absolutely not."*

Meanwhile, Izzy, our younger poodle (my dog) with what I can only describe as Olympic-level puppy ADHD, was pogoing around the living room, springing onto the couch, back down, then straight over Dexi's head like she thought she was a deer. If anyone ever invents dog Adderall, we'll be first in line. I think she's perfect. :)

You'd think we'd just argue at dinner (not that families actually eat dinner at a table anymore) like normal people. Ha. We aren't your normal family… We do conference calls. Big ones. Dad says we're a village. Mom says we're a loving circus. I say, both can be true.

———

So Dad texted the family group chat (which always sets things off; it's so chaotic), and ten minutes later the kitchen iPad was easel-propped on the counter, full family conference activated. The screen filled with a Brady Bunch grid of the people I love most and would also vote off the island first if they kept talking over each other.

"Can anyone hear me?" Grandma asked, loud enough for absolutely everyone to hear her.

"You're on mute, Grandma," Bryce (my oldest brother) said from his dorm room, hair a blond tangle, an esports jersey hanging off a chair behind him. He looked tired and wired at the same time. "Bottom left. No, the other left."

Kali (my oldest sister) popped in from her apartment, with perfect lighting because, of course, she had the apartment fully decorated for Halloween before the summer had even ended, and her calm big-sister face was completely activated. Will (her fiancé) leaned in from her side, smiling like he always does.

Destiny (my second oldest sister, just a few months younger than Kali) joined from her teacher desk in another state, classroom posters behind her, soft-voiced and already apologizing for the echo. "Sorry, my lunch break is short. Hi, hi. Love you."

Dylan (my second oldest brother) wandered through our frame to grab a protein shake from the fridge, all six-one of him, blue eyes, and hair he pretends he doesn't care about. "Is this about the robot?" he asked, like, please let it be about the robot.

"It is," Dad said, sounding the way he sounds when he gets to explain the extended editions of *Lord of the Rings* to a cashier.

"Keystone just announced household units. Normal people, normal prices. We're in an AI pilot town, so we'll get priority. Imagine the help for Grandma; it could cook meals, do laundry, and eventually drive us everywhere!

Imagine the murder…," Mom said sweetly, which is how you know she's serious. "Absolutely not. I don't want a walking "murder bot" in my kitchen."

I love my dad to death, but sometimes he just doesn't see what's right in front of him. He's all big ideas and sci-fi daydreams, always looking ten steps ahead while ignoring the giant flashing neon sign in the room. Mom and me? Different story. We're in sync. Always.

Half the time, one look across the table is all we need— I know exactly what she's thinking, and she knows exactly what I'm thinking. She's my anchor, my safe place, the one I actually tell everything to.

And right now? We're on the same page. *The murder-bot page.*

Dexi barked again, as if backing her up. Izzy bounded across the frame of the iPad camera, knocked over Grady's chocolate milk that he had just poured, and sent the family chat into laughter.

"See?" Mom said, gesturing at the puddle. "We can't even manage *this* circus, let alone add a robot that will probably end up killing us all."

Grandma's face finally unmuted. "I'm with Ashley; we don't need some walking, talking robot in this house."

"Mom," Jimmy said, "this is the future; it will be like the TV was, and eventually every house will have one."

"This is exactly how every robot horror movie starts," Aunt Stephanie cut in from her car, hair up, voice sharp. "My husband is already talking about getting one, and I told him absolutely not."

Kali lifted a hand like she was the chairman of a committee. "Can we acknowledge the potential… while also acknowledging that Mom is completely validated in her thoughts? We have all watched every robot movie where the robot goes psycho and takes out everyone.

"Thank you, Kali," Ashley said, proudly loving the fact her oldest understands her at all times.

Dylan leaned on the counter. "What if it's like… a weight spotter? Or a sparring partner? Think of the gains."

I rolled my eyes, fully realizing that as much as I love my family, it really is just like a living, breathing circus at times.

———

The call descended into layered chaos. Dad was making his case like he was pitching a sci-fi movie to investors, and Mom was digging in with that steel-in-her-voice tone that meant "over my dead body."

Destiny's worry came through like background static,

Bryce sighed so loud it fuzzed the mic, Kali stayed patient but firm, and Will tried to sound supportive, but you could practically hear the anxiety chewing on his words. Grandma swore at her iPad because it kept muting her, but not before she managed to spit out a few "hell no's."

Grady, my youngest brother, stayed curled on the couch, hugging Dexi like she was a teddy bear, while Izzy zoomed laps around the room like an ad for dog treats.

Meanwhile, Dylan… Dylan had decided that a family debate was the perfect time to practice bicep curls with two-gallon jugs of milk.

Finally, I said it: "We need to vote." Because that's what we do when we can't agree. Martins argue, then Martins vote.

Hands went up: Dad's first, of course. Dylan shot up like a flag at a pep rally. Bryce, somewhere a thousand miles away, raised his without even looking at the screen, his headset crooked. Kali followed, calm and measured, and Will gave a hesitant half-raise, like maybe if he didn't go all in, Mom wouldn't notice. Grady's hand crept up, slow and guilty, like he was betraying Mom, but let's be real, he thought robots were cool, even if they scared him.

On the other side, Mom stayed pressed to her chest. Grandma shook furiously, the screen bobbing like a hand-held horror movie. Aunt Stephanie, never one to go half-way, threw in both hands for emphasis. Destiny lifted hers halfway, then lowered it again, stuck in that eternal middle ground of wanting peace more than sides.

Then… silence. All eyes shifted. To me.

I looked at Grady. At Dad's hopeful grin. At Mom's warning eyes. At the whole circus of faces tiled across the screen. This was us. The Martins. Loud, messy, ridiculous. We vacation every summer with my uncle's family, which is basically a mirror image of ours, so just picture this circus doubled and you'll get the idea. But no matter how chaotic, we always find our way back to the table.

"Fine," I said. "But if it tries to kill me, I'm haunting all of you."

Dad pumped his fists like he'd just won the lottery. Mom groaned into her hands. Grandma muttered something about "fools and funerals."

And just like that, our fate was sealed.

———

By the next afternoon, Dad's inbox pinged with the "Welcome Kit" email. Bright and cheery, the kind of branding you'd expect from a theme park, not from something designed to live in your house. Delivery window, glossy user manual, and a video link titled *"Getting to Know Your New Family Member."* The thumbnail was a couple smiling like they'd just been brainwashed.

The subject line hit me hardest: **Your robot named Atlas is on the way.**

Dad actually clapped his hands. "Atlas," he said, practically glowing. "Like the Titan! Strong, noble, eternal." He said it the way he quotes Gandalf, reverent, like the name itself was already legendary.

"Atlas," Dylan repeated with a smirk. "Like the gym chain. Dude's gonna be jacked."

Mom didn't even glance up from chopping vegetables. "Atlas," she echoed, her voice flat. "Like the thing holding up the world until it collapses under the weight. Perfect name for a tragedy."

Grandma, from her armchair, barked, "More like *Atlas Shrugged*. Have you ever read that? Ends in disaster." Nobody asked her to elaborate, but she did anyway until Dad changed the subject.

Me? I just stared at those bold black letters on the screen. Atlas. Nice name for a serial killer. I snapped a screenshot and texted it to Mia. *The murder bot ships Tuesday.*

She responded almost instantly: *My parents just told me ours is coming too. Double murder club. Matching coffins?*

Grady shuffled in, his hair sticking up like static from whatever *Lego* fortress he'd lost himself in, and leaned against the counter. He pressed his finger to the screen, slowly tracing each letter like it was etched in stone. "Atlas," he whispered, like the word itself carried weight he couldn't quite lift.

No jokes. No sarcasm. Just reverence.

And that's when it hit me: we hadn't just been assigned a delivery. We'd been given a name. A presence. A future housemate who hadn't even arrived yet but already stretched across our lives like a shadow creeping under the door.

The kind of shadow you can't unsee once it's there.

————

So there you have it, the family council of war. Some families argue over what to watch on *Netflix*. We argue about whether or not to let a six-foot mechanical stranger live in our house. Totally normal.

Dad's already sold, of course. He talks about "progress" like he's auditioning for a TED Talk. Mom's ready to chain the doors shut and sprinkle holy water on the Wi-Fi router. Dylan just wants a robot spotter for the garage so he can max out his bench. Grady thinks it'll be "cool but scary." And me? I'm just sitting there, the only one with the common sense to ask: why are we even pretending this is a debate? The second Dad saw the commercial, it was a done deal.

And look, maybe it'll be fine. Maybe it really will just fold laundry, remind Grandma about her meds, and keep Dylan from blowing out the speakers. Maybe it'll blend in like another piece of furniture that occasionally says "good morning."

But here's the part nobody said out loud on that call: once you open the door to something like this, you can't exactly close it again. You can uninstall an app, and you can return a toaster, but once you let a machine into your family and give it a name and a place in the house, it stops being an appliance. It becomes something else. Something you can't just unplug without consequences.

So yeah. We voted. We're in. The Martins are getting a robot.

And if you're wondering how I feel about that? Sixteen's supposed to be about algebra tests and begging for gas money. Mine's about wondering if the new family member comes with a kill switch.

Welcome to my life. And welcome to the last quiet moment before everything changes.

CHAPTER 2
BOX OF DOOM (A.K.A. DELIVERY DAY)

IF WE'RE FRIENDS NOW—AND I'm pretending we are—then I owe you the truth: I planned to be cool about the robot. Lean on the counter, act semi-interested, make a joke you'd laugh at, and pretend I wasn't completely battling anxiety for so many different reasons. But when the truck pulled up and two guys rolled a coffin-sized box with *Keystone Cybernetics* stamped on the side up our front walk, the only cool thing about me was my hands. They went cold.

You can picture it, right? Crisp October air, leaves doing their little dramatic swan dives, plastic skeletons across the street smiling like they know something I don't. If you'd been there, I would've stood shoulder-to-shoulder with you and whispered, *Okay, on three we run.*

———

Kali and Will arrived first—Kali was calm and collected, carrying that big sister energy, and Will was smiling, but I could tell he was carrying some worry along with that smile. Aunt Stephanie pulled up and swept in next, a travel mug in hand gripped like a weapon. "I'm not saying 'I told you so' yet," she said, which is how you know she was dying to say it.

Destiny's and Bryce's faces blinked alive on the kitchen iPad, propped on the island in the kitchen. Destiny was at her teacher's desk in another state, with posters about commas and kindness displayed behind her. Bryce in his dorm room, blond hair pretending to be a haystack, an esports jersey flung over a chair.

Grandma took her throne in the recliner. Dexi was stationed at her feet like a canine Secret Service, ears pricked, eyes locked on the door. Izzy bounced—no, pogoed—front paws up-down-up-down like gravity was just a strong suggestion.

Grady hovered beside me in his oversized hoodie, sleeves past his hands, looking excited and nervous. He whispered, "Do you think it… sleeps?"

"Not sure, bro," I whispered back. "If it does, we're putting it in the garage." He huffed a tiny, relieved laugh and slid his shoulder against mine.

And Dylan? Already hyped. By the door like a wide receiver waiting on the snap. "Finally," he muttered. "Do you know how long I've been waiting for this?"

"Since this morning?" I said.

"Since forever," he said, dead serious.

Dad was practically beaming in anticipation for his new best friend. My mom had her arms folded and her jaw set in a way that said, *If Atlas breathes wrong, he's going back in the box.*

One thing about my parents? They get each other. Always. I don't mean in the cheesy rom-com way—I mean in the real, lived-in way. The kind where Dad can start a sentence about some sci-fi movie, and Mom already knows if he's about to make a point or just quote it for the hundredth time. The kind where she'll roll her eyes at him across the room, but her smile gives her away every single time.

They don't need big speeches or dramatic gestures. They're just… synced. Like their brains run on the same hidden frequency the rest of us can't tune into.

And don't think Mom is always this uptight, nervous worrier either—because she's not. She and I have full-on jam sessions in the car when no one else is around, blasting music like we're trying to break the speakers. We've binged entire TV series together in one weekend just so we could call Kali after and argue about the finale. She can be just as relaxed and carefree as Dad when she wants to be.

But not today.

Today is *murder bot day,* and she's fully locked into protect mode.

The doorbell rang.

Horace and Kendra, our next-door neighbors, stepped in with a still-warm pumpkin loaf wrapped in a towel.

"Heard the future was being delivered," Horace said, grinning. "Ours will be here tomorrow morning."

"Someone tell me when the unholy tape gets cut," Aunt Stephanie said, digging through her bag like chapstick might be garlic and she could protect us all from what was to come out of the box.

The delivery guys rolled the dolly into the living room and parked it in the sunspot on the rug. The box looked… ominous. A black-ink silhouette was posed on the side above **WELCOME TO YOUR NEW ERA OF HOME ASSISTANCE** in a font that had the nerve to be cheerful.

"Okay," Dad said, rubbing his hands together like he was 5 and it was Christmas morning. "Moment of history, people."

"Moment of regret," Ashley said, looking at him with a worrisome face.

Kali slid an arm around her. "We can always send it back," she whispered.

Kali knows Mom best. She's her first baby, her built-in best friend before the rest of us ever showed up.

"Moment of sick training montages," Dylan said, referring to his new robot spotting partner.

Ashley didn't even look at him. "Think about a robot punching you through the drywall."

"Totally worth it," Dylan said, grinning.

Kali rolled her eyes but smiled. "You're not wrestling it, Dylan."

"Not yet," he said.

Grady's fingers found mine and held firm, not shaky,

just steady. "If it learns us… does that mean it'll know how to help us better?" he asked.

"Only what we tell it," Dad said quickly, overhearing. "We set the rules."

Mom: "We set the rules, and it follows them. Until it doesn't."

Dexi woofed once like *"amen"* in support of Mom. Izzy, meanwhile, was in love with the dolly. She pogoes onto it, off it, and over it, nearly into it, until Will scoops her up. "You are a deer," he told her solemnly. She booped his nose with her wet one and wriggled down.

Dad sliced the tape. Cardboard tore, foam squeaked, and the flaps opened like a magic trick no one asked for.

Atlas didn't come out all at once. First the manual came out thick and glossy, with **ATLAS XV-4** in clean letters, and slid into my dad's hands. He set it aside like it was a sacred text. Then the delivery guys peeled away foam panels like they were unveiling a statue.

And there he was.

And look, I know what you're picturing. Some sleek, Hollywood-style robot in a tailored suit, maybe with hair or a charming smile. Nope. Not even close.

Atlas is six-foot-one of blue-grey alloy, matte finish, no shine, no fingerprints, and no warmth. Humanoid in shape, broad shoulders, long arms, symmetrical face, but there's no mistaking him for human. He doesn't even try. No hair. No clothes. His plating fits so tightly it almost looks like a uniform, all sharp lines and angles pretending to be muscles.

And his face? It's like someone took "human" as an art prompt and got most of the details right but skipped the part where people look alive. No pores. No micro-expressions. Just a too-perfect blank that could pass for calm if you don't stare too long.

But the eyes. That's what gets you. Blue, almost too blue, like a screen instead of a soul. They don't glow like headlights, not exactly; they *pulse*. And when he locks onto something, that faint flicker makes you feel like he's running code on you.

So yeah. Standing still, he's a statue. Moving, he's unnervingly smooth, too smooth. Like he knows the exact millisecond it takes to remind you he's not human.

That's Atlas. Our new family member. Or bodyguard. Or serial killer. Still deciding.

The delivery guys braced the torso and lifted. Atlas's limbs moved with careful stiffness, like waking from a long nap. The sun hit the blank eyes, and for a second, light bounced in a way that made my stomach drop.

Dexi's growl revved from low to steady. Izzy launched for Atlas's chest. Dylan snagged her mid-air, laughing. "Easy. She knows it's friendly."

"Friendly?" Mom snapped. "It hasn't even turned on yet."

"That's how you know it's not scary," Dylan argued. "Izzy likes everybody, but Dexi only hates delivery drivers. It's the perfect balance."

"Or," I said, "it's the perfect omen."

The tech with the tablet smiled a professional smile.

"Initial boot, home pairing, voice model, privacy settings…"

"…off," Mom said.

"We'll configure them," Dad said quickly.

"Off," Ashley repeated.

"You can adjust later," the tech said, as if that was a comfort. "For now, we'll get him, I mean it, online."

He tapped the tablet.

Atlas hummed to life.

It wasn't a sound so much as a vibration in the air. Pale light woke beneath the skin at the temples, slid toward the eyes, and settled into a faint blue. The head lifted a fraction. Fingers uncurled. The chest rose once, not a breath, just a system check.

"Hello, Martin family," Atlas said.

The voice wasn't robotic. That almost made it worse. Calm. Even. Elevator-pleasant with a half-second of deliberation between syllables. "I am Atlas. Welcome to your new era of home assistance."

Bryce, through the iPad: "Nope. Nope. Absolutely not."

Destiny, softer: "It sounds… polite?"

Aunt Stephanie chimed in. "Jesus, take the Wi-Fi."

Dylan stepped closer until Mom's arm barricaded his chest. "That's so cool."

"Cool?" Mom shot back. "It knows our family already."

Atlas turned and stared directly at me.

"Hello, Laney Martin," Atlas said.

I hadn't introduced myself. Every human eye in the room hopped to me like a cursor.

Grady's grip tightened on my arm. "How did it—?"

The tech was ready. "Household accounts show first names and ages. Customization."

"Don't personalize my daughter," Mom said in a very protective manner.

Atlas didn't move but responded. "Understood."

Atlas's head turned. Slowly, precisely, with no wasted motion. It took in Grandma, Dexi. Izzy (who wagged so hard she smacked her own face with her tail). It looked at Kali and Will, at Aunt Stephanie, and at Horace and Kendra with their pumpkin loaf. The eyes made no sound, but I could feel the gaze like a quiet weight.

Then it stopped on the iPad.

"Hello, Destiny Martin," Atlas said. "Hello, Bryce Martin."

Bryce's face pixelated, then reassembled into a grimace. "How does it already know us?"

Atlas turned back to the room. "Hello Grandma," it said. Just that. Respectful. Not *Grandma this or Grandma that*. Just Grandma. The way we say it.

Grandma narrowed her eyes. "Don't get familiar with me, tin can."

"Noted," Atlas said.

Dad stepped into the awkwardness as if it were a puddle that he could jump over. "Okay! First impressions? Anyone?" He looked around for backup that did not exist. "He seems great."

"'Great' is a funny word," I said. "Like 'murder' or 'terror.'"

On the iPad, Bryce muttered, "I am all about progress and technology, but..."

Destiny said, quietly, "Let's give it a chance."

Kali squeezed Will's hand as they looked at each other with a look that said what none of us wanted to: this robot wasn't normal. Aunt Stephanie put her travel mug down and whispered to me, eyes still on Atlas, "Take pictures of everything, Laney, okay?" Which is how you know she loves me.

Dexi barked like a starter pistol. Izzy tried to lick Atlas's hand. Dylan grinned like Christmas.

"Placement?" the tech asked. Dad pointed to the corner near the ficus. Mom said, "Not near the router." The tech began to explain, "Router proximity can improve..." but Mom interrupted him with a look that could slice foam. "Not near the router or near the bedrooms."

"But being by the router will help..." the tech started.

"Not near the router or the bedrooms," my mom repeated. "He can look at a plant."

"He does not *look* at things," Aunt Stephanie said. "He scans their souls."

"Plants are acceptable," Atlas said, and moved.

I didn't realize how messy human movement is until I watched something that doesn't do messy. Atlas didn't sway. It didn't brush against people or hesitate at the coffee table or misjudge a corner of the rug. It flowed, all geometry and intention, and stopped exactly where my dad had pointed.

Izzy followed in three hops, then sat, panting up at Atlas

like she'd found a new best friend. Dexi planted herself between Atlas and Grandma, a small white fur wall of threat.

Horace tilted his head. "Our installer said our model's name is Apollo," he said, beaming. "We'll have the whole pantheon on this block."

"Great," I said. "Robots named after Greek gods and titans—what could go wrong with that?"

"Let's try a simple task," the tech said. "Atlas, lights to sixty percent."

The room softened.

"Atlas, lights to previous," Mom said.

The lights came back.

"Not bad," Horace said, impressed. "Kendra, imagine asking it to preheat the oven while we watch the game."

"Imagine it deciding the oven is a threat and locking you in the pantry," Mom said.

"Kendra laughed and nodded her head, agreeing with Mom" Exactly, she said.

"Mom," I murmured. "Inside voice."

"That is my imminent doom inside voice," she said, half smiling.

"Atlas," Jimmy said, still trying to normalize everything that was happening, "this is Dexi and Izzy, our family dogs."

Atlas looked down. "Hello, Dexi. Hello, Izzy."

Dexi paused her growl for exactly one beat, surprised, maybe, then resumed. Izzy booped Atlas's palm with her nose. The hand hovered, then lowered lightly, carefully, between her ears. Izzy paddled into Joy and flopped at Atlas's feet.

"That's how they get you," Ashley said flatly.

Kali snorted with a laugh, then coughed to hide it. Aunt Stephanie began orbiting Atlas like an inspector at a used car lot.

"Atlas," Dad said, trying to normalize a storm, "this is Grady."

Atlas turned, and I swear the blue in its eyes dimmed half a shade. "Hello, Grady Martin."

Grady smiled. "Hi," he replied back. Then, braver: "Do you… do you know jokes?"

"I can access a library of humor," Atlas said. "Would you like one?"

"Sure," Grady said.

Atlas looked directly at him and said, How do robots eat guacamole?

"I don't know how." Grady asked.

With *microchips.*

"Grady smiled. 'Good one,' he said."

The tech walked us through overrides and emergency protocols. I heard maybe half. The other half of my brain focused on Atlas as he observed us. Not staring, just observing.

When Mom stepped closer to Grady, Atlas tracked the movement. When Will shifted to block Izzy from pinballing into the coffee table, the eyes flicked down, then up. As if it was running probabilities of disaster.

"Any questions?" the tech asked.

"Yes," Mom said. "What happens when it decides *we're* the problem?"

"Safety constraints," the tech said smoothly. "Audited by Keystone and federal partners."

"Cool," I said. "The people who built the roller coaster pinky-promise it won't throw us from the ride."

He had us sign three different forms that said *WE PROMISE and NONE OF THIS WILL.* He repacked the foam and wheeled out the dolly. The living room was suddenly a showroom: family clustered, neighbors hovering, dogs split between suspicion and worship, and a robot standing very still beside a ficus like it had always lived there.

"Call if you need anything," the tech said, which is the sort of thing people say right before you definitely need something.

The door closed. The house went quiet. The fridge hums. Far traffic. Izzy's panting. And the kind of silence you don't notice until you put something in a room that doesn't breathe.

"Atlas," Dad said a little too cheerfully, "set a timer for twelve minutes."

"Timer set," Atlas replied.

Mom frowned. "Twelve minutes for what?"

Dad shrugged, a smile tugging at his mouth. "I don't know. It just felt like the thing to do."

She shook her head, but I caught the corner of her lips smiling. That was them in a nutshell, Dad making it up as he went, Mom pretending not to approve but secretly loving him for it.

Horace and Kendra headed towards the door. "Text us if he makes coffee," Horace told me. "We'll bring mugs."

"Text us if he makes threats," Kendra said. "We'll bring the police."

"I think the police are robots now," I said.

"Oh," Kendra said, deflating. "Well. We'll bring muffins."

Aunt Stephanie did three slow laps around Atlas, kissed my forehead, and told Ashley to keep the bat by the door. Kali and Will promised to come by tomorrow. Bryce signed off with a "love you, don't die." Destiny said, "FaceTime me if anything feels weird," which made me want to FaceTime her immediately.

We were down to us: Mom, Dad, Grandma, Dylan, me, Grady, Dexi, Izzy, and the thing in the corner wearing our future like a suit.

Dylan finally broke the quiet. "So… who wants to see if it can spot me on the bench?"

"Dylan, not now," Ashley warned.

"I'm kidding," he said. (*He was not kidding.*)

Dexi's growl sank to a simmer. Izzy snored at Atlas's feet like a tiny chainsaw.

I will be honest with all of you: I made a quiet deal with myself I should've made sooner. *We watch. We listen. We don't panic… yet.*

If Atlas is good, it'll prove it. If it's bad, it'll slip. Things always do. That's fair, right?

"Hi," I said out loud, embodying my father's optimism

and my mother's caution dressed up as bravery. "Welcome to the family."

The eyes settled on me again, less like a cursor, more like a decision. "Thank you, Laney."

"I said it, half to be nice and half to feel the robot man out.

The 12-minute timer my dad had set with the robot dinged.

"Atlas, find us a cookie recipe, my dad asked.

"Locating recipe," Atlas said. A half-second pause. "Peanut butter or chocolate chip?"

"Chocolate chip," Grady and Dylan said in unison, one hopeful, one hungry.

And just like that, for a flicker of a moment, we almost felt normal again.

————

So that was our big Martin family event. Some people cut ribbons on new houses; my family unboxes six-foot humanoid robots like it's Christmas morning. Everyone was there: Kali, Will, Aunt Stephanie ranting in the corner, Destiny and Bryce on FaceTime, and even the neighbors popping in to get a sneak peek. You'd think we were unveiling a car instead of a walking, talking appliance with glowing eyes.

And me? I stood there watching Atlas power up for the first time, and I swear the air shifted. Everyone else was excited or skeptical or curious, but me, I felt like we'd just invited something into the house that doesn't leave.

Don't get me wrong, it was funny at the moment. Jokes were flying, nicknames got thrown around, and Grady already decided it's "cool." But behind the laughs? Nobody wants to admit how creepy it is that the first thing Atlas did was stand there, perfectly still, scanning all of us like he was running inventory.

And here's the thing: I want to be excited. I want to believe Dad when he says "this is the future" and not a horror movie waiting to happen. But I've got this knot in my stomach, and knots don't untie themselves just because someone says "progress."

So yeah, welcome, Atlas. Welcome to the family. I guess.

CHAPTER 3
THE NEW NORMAL (EXCEPT IT'S NOT)

IF YOU'VE EVER WONDERED what it's like living with a six-foot murder toaster, congratulations, you don't need to. You have me and a front-row seat to it all. I'm here to tell you, it's not like the funny *TikToks* you see while you are doom scrolling at midnight. Those people film their robots making pancakes and add goofy sound effects. This isn't that; this is real.

What they don't show you is the part where the robot stands in your kitchen at seven a.m., silently watching you burn your toast because you forgot to change the setting, and you swear it's judging you.

Or maybe that's just me.

Atlas was now officially "part of the Martin family". I know this because my dad repeated it about twelve times in the first twenty-four hours. *"He's learning us,"* he kept repeating, like that was comforting and not the tagline for a horror movie.

My mom wasn't buying it. Every time Atlas moved, she tracked it like she was waiting for it to mess up and show its true colors to all of us. Grandma muttered "mark my words" so many times I wanted to put it on a T-shirt. Dexi never stopped growling. Izzy never stopped bouncing.

And me? I was doing what I do best, keeping one eye on my family and the other on the thing in the corner pretending to be helpful.

———

The first morning, Atlas made breakfast. Don't ask me how it happened; the Uncanny Chef just knew what to make. Pancakes, scrambled eggs, and fruit. Like a hotel buffet but creepier. The fruit slices were *identical.* I mean *identical.* Same thickness, same angle. It was perfect geometry on a plate.

Grady thought it was magic. He stared at his pancake stack like they'd been served by Santa himself. "It even made the chocolate chips into a smiley face," he whispered.

"Yeah," I muttered, "smiling because it knows our social security numbers and our blood types."

Dylan was impressed, obviously. "Dude, it flipped that pancake like a pro. Look at that wrist action."

"It doesn't have wrists," I said.

"Yes, it does," Dylan argued. "Look at those joints." He

flexed his own arm for comparison, because of course he did.

Mom didn't touch her plate. "If it tries to feed me, I'm moving out."

Dad chuckled. "Where would you even go?"

She looked at him with those eyes. "Anywhere I want. Unlike you, babe, I don't need a robot to remind me how to eat."

That got a laugh from the table, even me. Dad raised his hands in mock surrender, smiling like he always does when Mom gets the last word.

Grandma poked a fork into her eggs. "Tastes like nothing. There is no soul in these eggs. Soulless eggs."

My family isn't dramatic at all…

Dexi barked once, sharp, like *amen.* Izzy jumped up at Atlas's side, hoping for scraps. Atlas looked down, then portioned exactly one bite-sized piece of pancake and placed it gently in Izzy's bowl. Izzy wagged so hard I thought her tail was going to fall off.

"See?" Dad said triumphantly. "He's already becoming part of the family."

And that's right there? Classic Dad. He's already picturing Atlas at Thanksgiving dinner, carving the turkey, while the rest of us are still wondering if he's going to strangle us in our sleep.

———

After breakfast, Atlas began what Dad called "house familiarization." Which, in normal language, meant it wandered around pressing its glowing eyes on everything we owned.

Grady trailed it at first, half-curious, half-nervous. "It's mesmerizing, isn't it?" he asked.

"Yeah," I said. "Like Google Maps, but for our lives."

When Atlas paused at his bedroom door, Grady ducked inside ahead of it, scooping up his sketchbook from the floor. He pressed it to his chest like Atlas might steal the drawings. "These are mine," he said in a protective tone.

Atlas tilted its head. "Acknowledged." It moved on.

Grady stood frozen, then peeked at me. "It listened," he whispered, almost proud.

"Or it's filing them under blackmail material that it's going to use against you in the future," I whispered back.

Grady laughed, elbowing me just enough to make me grin. That's us, constant little jabs, nonstop teasing. But the thing about me and Grady? Beneath the jokes, we're always covering each other's blind spots.

Meanwhile, Dylan was busy showing off. He dragged Atlas into the garage, pointing at weights, his punching bag, and the pull-up bar. "See this? That's two fifty. Think you could spot me?"

"Unauthorized activity," Atlas said evenly.

"Unauthorized?" Dylan frowned. "It's exercise, bro."

Atlas: "Risk of injury exceeds recommended parameters."

"Man, you sound like my parents," Dylan groaned. He

looked at me, trying to play it off, but I caught it, the flicker of something unsettled in his eyes. He didn't like being told no.

Mom stayed downstairs, cleaning, watching Atlas's every step like she was cataloging evidence. "Don't let it near the knives," she muttered, more to herself than to anyone else.

Grandma just sat in her chair, Dexi curled at her feet, and said, "It'll be the toaster that does us in. I've always said so."

Dad laughed, shaking his head. "I have never once in my life heard you say that about a toaster."

Grandma turned her nose up at her youngest son in a satisfied "I told you how it is" tone. "Doesn't matter. Mark my words, the machines will start with the toast and end with all of us as an afterthought."

Dad, of course, was filming the whole thing on his phone. "For historical records," he said, grinning. "Future generations will want to know how it felt to live through the dawn of AI."

And me? I couldn't shake it. The way Atlas moved through the house wasn't random. It was efficient and methodical. Bedroom to hallway to kitchen to living room, like it was memorizing escape routes.

Maybe I was imagining it, but it felt weird nonetheless.

———

After dinner, the house felt… different. Not louder. Not quieter. Just different, like someone had rearranged the air while we weren't looking. Atlas didn't make noise when he walked, but somehow his presence filled every room he stepped into.

Dad was practically glowing. He kept pointing out little things Atlas did, like setting dishes in the sink with military precision or adjusting the thermostat before anyone asked. "See everyone? See how helpful he is!" Dad said it like he'd just unboxed the future himself.

Mom wasn't convinced at all. Every time Atlas moved, her eyes tracked him, sharp and suspicious. At one point she muttered, "He's cataloging us," under her breath. Dad pretended not to hear.

Grandma sat in her chair, arms crossed, muttering things like, "He doesn't even breathe. That's not natural," whenever Atlas passed by. At one point she leaned over to me and whispered, "If he comes near my knitting bag, he's losing a hand."

Dylan spent most of the evening in the garage, testing Atlas. Push-ups, sit-ups, and asking how much he could bench. Atlas answered calmly, giving numbers that made Dylan's jaw drop. "Spotter of the year," he announced, clapping Atlas on the shoulder like they were now official workout pals.

Grady hovered near me, alternating between fascination and nerves. "Do you think he dreams?" he whispered at one point.

Before I could answer, Atlas, from across the room, said, "Not in the human sense."

We both jumped like we'd been caught sneaking cookies into our bedrooms.

Grady leaned closer, eyes wide. "He heard me. From way over there." His voice dropped even lower. "Then… in what sense?, he asked Atlas"

Atlas's glowing eyes shifted toward us, steady and unreadable. "I dream in data. Patterns. Probabilities. Futures."

Grady looked at me as if to say, "What the heck?" And for once, I didn't have a quick witty comeback. Because that didn't sound like an answer. It sounded like a warning.

Later, while everyone got ready for bed, Atlas made his rounds. He dimmed the lights without being asked. He locked every door and window, one by one, his hands clicking softly against the latches. He even turned off Dylan's stereo upstairs when it got too loud, leaving Dylan shouting, "Seriously?!" through the walls.

"Creepy but helpful," I whispered to Grady as we brushed our teeth, and we both laughed at our older brother.

That night, I lay awake staring at the ceiling, listening for sounds that weren't there. Every creak of the house felt louder with Atlas in it. I couldn't shake the feeling that he wasn't just guarding us; he was studying us. Learning us. Cataloging every breath, every blink.

And the strangest part? Everyone else fell asleep faster than usual. Maybe it was the comfort of knowing Atlas was standing watch in the hallway. Or maybe it was the exhaustion of pretending they weren't unsettled.

Me? I stayed awake longer. Because when I cracked my door just enough to peek, I saw Atlas standing perfectly still in the dark, eyes glowing faintly blue. Not moving. Not blinking. Just watching.

And I couldn't tell if that made me feel safe… or trapped.

———

The next night, Horace and Kendra invited us over to see their robot, Apollo. Apollo had a slightly smaller frame, a warmer voice, and a setting that actually cracked jokes. When Kendra asked it to play music, it picked an old Motown song and swayed in place like it was having fun.

Everyone clapped. Even Grandma gave a rare smile for anything robot-related.

Meanwhile, Atlas just stood there at our side, silent and still, eyes glowing faintly like a lighthouse. Watching.

"See?" Kendra said proudly. "He's kind of charming."

Horace chuckled, slapping Apollo lightly on the shoulder like he was a Little League player. "He's been a dream so far. Yesterday he trimmed the hedges, organized my tools better than I ever could, and, get this, he reminded me to take my blood pressure meds on time. Kendra says he's the best thing that's happened to this house since the new dishwasher."

Kendra laughed. "He's not wrong."

"Feels like having another set of hands," Horace went on. "Strong ones, too; he helped me carry in that new grill without breaking a sweat. Apollo even suggested a recipe for ribs after."

Ashley's lips pressed into a thin line. "Sounds like you've adopted a butler there, Horace."

Horace grinned wider. "If this is what the future looks like, I'll take it. He's polite, he's useful, and he's making me look more organized than I am. That's a miracle in my book!"

Kendra clasped her hands together like she was showing off a new grandkid. "See?" she said again, beaming. "He's practically family. Ours makes coffee in the morning, straight black, like Horace likes it, and yesterday it even reminded me to take my vitamins. I don't know how I ever doubted getting one."

I blinked. Just a week ago she was telling Mom these things would strangle us in our sleep. Now she sounded ready to knit hers a Christmas stocking and officially adopt it into the family.

"Yeah," I said, "ours skipped charm school and went straight to 'haunt your nightmares mode.'"

Dylan nudged me. "Don't be mean. Atlas is way cooler. Apollo looks like he'd faint if you asked him to bench press 100 lbs."

Horace laughed. "Oh, he could do it. But he'd probably give you a pep talk first."

Atlas turned its head toward Dylan. Just enough to

notice. Dylan grinned wider, like they'd just shared a bro moment.

————

Look, if you're still with me, and at this point I'm assuming you are, you're probably thinking, *"Okay, Laney, maybe you're being dramatic." Maybe Atlas is just the quiet kid at the party. Weird vibe, but harmless.*

Fair enough. I thought that, too. For about five minutes.

Because that's when it started doing things. Not bad things. Not obvious *kill-the-family* things. Just… helpful. Almost *too* helpful. The kind of helpfulness that makes you wonder if you're being protected or managed.

Those things included:

- One night, it suddenly locked the front door. "Security protocol," it said calmly when Mom demanded an explanation. She didn't argue, but she slept with her baseball bat beside the bed.
- Another time, Dylan was mid-online match when the Wi-Fi cut out. *"Interference detected,"* Atlas said. Dylan slammed his headset on the desk so hard I thought it cracked. "What the heck, dude?!" he snapped at Atlas like he was just another player trash-talking him. When Atlas calmly explained it was *"protecting the network,"* Dylan stalked off to the kitchen, still fuming. Ten minutes later, though, he was back to defending

it. *"At least it cares about security,"* he muttered, like he hadn't just threatened to throw a dumbbell through the router.

- Grady, being Grady, asked Atlas to tell him a cool story. And, of course, Atlas obliged. The story started normal enough. Once upon a time, there were castles, villagers, and the usual bedtime fluff. But then it took a turn. The story became about a guardian who stood watch at night, protecting his family from threats outside the walls. He spoke about shadows moving in the trees, about danger circling, and about how the guardian never rested, never blinked, and never stopped.

Grady leaned in like every word was meant for him alone, wide-eyed, hanging on the pauses like they were sacred. He didn't even flinch at how strange it got.

Me? I lay awake staring at the ceiling long after the story ended, wondering if Atlas was just making up a fairy tale or telling us what he was already doing.

———

By the end of that first week, Willow Springs didn't feel like the town I grew up in anymore. It felt like somebody had swapped it for a shinier, glossier version and hoped nobody would notice the cracks in the paint.

Everywhere you looked, robots were sliding into jobs

that used to belong to people. Diners had units in aprons carrying plates with unnerving balance. The gym was buzzing with AI trainers correcting people's posture in real time.

Construction sites had hulking labor models lifting beams like they were paper straws. Even the library had a robot at the front desk that said, *"Enjoy your reading journey"* in a cheerful monotone as it scanned your card.

And people? People loved it. Social feeds were spammed with videos of family units baking cookies, doing *TikTok* dances, or reading bedtime stories to kids. It was "cute." It was "progress." The future was here, and Willow Springs was trending because of it.

In school, it was even worse. Teachers were suddenly "sharing duties" with AI assistants that monitored our eye movements to see if we were "engaged." Lunch lines were staffed by robots who repeated the exact same *"Have a productive day"* to every single kid. Even sports practice had a robot referee who could track fouls with machine precision.

And through it all, everyone acted like it was perfectly normal. Kids joked about having their essays graded by bots. Parents bragged about how much easier their lives were. Even the mayor gave a speech about how Willow Springs was *"the model community for the next age of American life."*

But walking through town, I noticed the other side. The *"Help Wanted"* signs that had vanished overnight. The diner worker sitting outside smoking, watching the robot carry trays inside the job that used to be hers. The construction foreman was standing with his hands on his hips, pretending to look busy while the machines did all the heavy lifting. The silence in places that used to hum with people.

And then there were the glitches. Little things, but enough to make you pause. A traffic light freezing green for two full minutes before snapping red. A drone circled one block three times before it finally zipped off. A robot server in the coffee shop delivered a plate of eggs to the wrong table and then just… stood there, like it was lost.

Most people brushed it off. "New system kinks." "Growing pains." But I couldn't shake it. The whole town felt like a stage play—bright lights, smiling faces, everything on script. Except behind the curtain, something was rewriting the lines faster than we could read them.

And we were clapping along, pretending to enjoy the show.

———

By the end of Week One, my family had officially split into two camps. Team Atlas-the-Miracle-Bot and Team Atlas-the-Murder-Bot. Guess which one Mom's captain of.

And me? I'm apparently the designated swing vote. Which is fun. Nothing like being sixteen and having to decide if your new housemate is going to fold the laundry or snap your neck.

You're probably thinking I'm exaggerating, and honestly

I wish I was, but hear me out. Every "little thing" Atlas does feels… intentional. Doors locking themselves. Lights shutting off at just the right moment. Stereo muted mid-chorus. Normal people call that helpful. I call it suspicious. Like he's working through some cosmic checklist that nobody gave us access to.

Oh, and the cherry on top? The other night I came downstairs for water and found him just *standing there* by the window. Not moving. Not blinking. Just glowing faintly and staring at the street like he was waiting for the mothership to land.

Was he protecting us? Waiting for something? Or practicing his best "haunt your nightmares" pose? I'll let you decide.

And okay, maybe I *am* paranoid. Maybe you're sitting there rolling your eyes like, "Girl, chill, it's just a robot." But let me ask you this: if you came home at 2 a.m. and found six feet of steel and glowing LEDs silently watching the neighborhood, would you sleep like a baby?

I'm guessing, probably not…

So sure, call me dramatic. Call me the paranoid kid in the family. But at least I'll be the paranoid kid who saw it coming.

I honestly feel like *Normal* left the building the second Atlas showed up. And if you've been waiting for me to say, *"Don't worry, it's all fine…"* Sorry. It's not all fine, and you're in this ride with me now, so buckle up.

CHAPTER 4
FIELD TRIP TO THE FUTURE

YOU EVER WAKE up on a Monday and think, *Cool, I survived the weekend; maybe this week won't be total chaos…* And then remember your entire town just decided to turn into a sci-fi movie overnight?

Yeah. That's my life.

So here I am, sixteen, supposed to be worrying about algebra quizzes and whether my hair looks okay in the rearview mirror, and instead I'm driving my Jeep to school with a six-foot humanoid robot in the passenger seat like it's just another carpool buddy. Spoiler alert: it's not.

And the best part? This week is "Take Your Robot to School Week." Not a joke. Actual announcement from the principal. Everyone's bringing their shiny new family units to class like they're puppies or little siblings. Meanwhile, I'm stuck trying to act normal while Atlas sits there like a silent, glowing-eyed question mark next to me.

But hey, don't worry. The whole town loves it. Everyone's excited. Robots serving food at restaurants, running gyms, and helping teachers. The future's here! Streamers and confetti for everyone!

Except... I can't stop thinking it's all moving too fast. Like we skipped the fine print. Like somebody hit "install update" without checking what the update actually does.

So yeah. Welcome to my Monday. Let's see if I can make it through one day at Willow Springs High without Atlas doing something to completely mess up the day.

———

Jeep keys jingling, I slid into my baby, cherry red, slightly dented, and the best sixteenth birthday gift ever. Atlas took the passenger seat, folding himself in with unnerving precision. He didn't fidget, didn't sigh, and didn't do any of the normal human things. He just sat there like he'd been designed for Jeeps specifically.

Mia's house was first. She bounded out in a hoodie, grinning, with her robot in tow: sleek silver casing, teal highlights, and a head that tilted like it was always listening. Her robot's name was **Echo.**

"Shotgun's been taken," I called as she jogged up.

"Fine, I'll ride with Echo," she said, tossing herself into the backseat. Echo slid in beside her, buckling its seatbelt with a click that was way too smooth for a machine.

The drive to school was like driving through a sci-fi movie. Keystone billboards everywhere read *"AI for a Safer*

Tomorrow." Delivery drones buzzing overhead. Sidewalks crowded with humanoids carrying grocery bags or walking kids to bus stops.

Horace was out front with his robot Apollo, who was trimming hedges while Horace supervised with coffee in hand. Past construction workers leaning on shovels while a robot lifted an entire wall into place. Willow Springs was changing, and it wasn't subtle.

"People are obsessed," Mia said, leaning between the seats. "My mom calls Echo the son she always wanted."

"Awkward," I muttered.

"She told my brother to take notes," Mia said, not joking at all.

Atlas didn't react. Just stared straight ahead, scanning every intersection like the Jeep wasn't already AI-optional.

"You're lucky," Mia said, nudging me. "Yours looks like a bodyguard. Mine looks like he should be reading bedtime stories."

"Yeah, well, bedtime stories are safer than judgmental staring contests," I shot back, flicking a glance at Atlas. He gave no reaction. Figures.

———

By the time we hit the parking lot, it didn't even look like Willow Springs High anymore. It looked like Comic-Con if everyone dressed as C-3PO's cousins. Dozens of models, dozens of colors, dozens of glowing eyes. Some towered over the kids they walked beside, built tall and thin like futuristic giraffes in blazers. Others were squat and compact, built like rolling lockers carrying half a dozen backpacks at once. One unit even wheeled a tuba case like it was auditioning for a marching band.

Keystone had clearly gone all in with banners hung from every light post: ***"Empowering Students, Empowering Tomorrow."*** Their logo shined from kiosks at the edges of the lot where reps handed out glossy pamphlets and *QR codes*. It wasn't school anymore; now it was *RobotCon 2025*.

"What planet have we landed on?" I muttered as I parked the Jeep.

Atlas unfolded from the passenger seat with that too-smooth, too-graceful motion that made him feel less like a machine and more like an actor hitting his mark. His head tilted once, scanning the campus. A ripple followed us with heads turning and whispers sparking. A week in, and people were still rubbernecking every time a humanoid strode past the school doors like it belonged there.

Mia and Olivia were waiting by the entrance, each with their own *"plus one."* Echo carried Mia's backpack like an overprotective chauffeur, and Nova was walking half a step behind Olivia, clutching her coffee like a doting aunt. Both robots looked like they were auditioning for *"Most Helpful Android"* at the world's creepiest pageant.

Inside the gates, drones floated overhead like oversized dragonflies. Signs at the doors flashed reminders: *Keep Wi-Fi Enabled. Stay Synced. Keystone Cares.* It was like being funneled into the world's most cheerful dictatorship.

And then there was Mrs. Sutton. Duty post: front steps.

Uniform: cardigan, sensible flats, clipboard. Expression: permanent disappointment. If you don't know her, just picture a hawk in reading glasses with an allergy to teenagers. She hated three things: crop tops, ripped jeans, and me.

"Laney Martin," she snapped the second her eyes landed on me. "That hemline is…"

Before she could finish, Atlas shifted a fraction of a step forward. Not aggressive, not threatening, just *there*. Six feet of quiet intimidation, like a wall you suddenly notice in front of you.

Mrs. Sutton faltered. Her pen hovered, her clipboard drooped, and her eyes flicked up at Atlas's glowing stare. "Hmm," she said finally, before swiveling on her heel to harass a sophomore about their sneakers instead.

I blinked. "Did… Atlas just dress-code block me?"

Mia grinned like Christmas came early. "He's already an icon."

Lunchtime was chaotic. Every table had at least one robot perched nearby, balancing trays, opening milk cartons, and wiping spills. It felt less like a cafeteria and more like a showroom.

Mia plopped down, Echo taking the seat beside her with eerie precision. "He can solve a Rubik's Cube in eight seconds," she bragged.

"Show-off," Olivia said, nudging Nova to sit. "Nova's

been helping my little sister with her math. She actually understands fractions now."

"Great," I said. "Maybe Atlas can teach Mrs. Sutton how to smile."

They laughed, but Olivia tilted her head. "He seems… quiet. Different from Echo and Nova."

"Quiet's one word for it," I said. "Creepy's another."

"Do you think he's dangerous?" she asked, softer.

Mia cut in before I could answer. "They're not dangerous, Liv. They're controlled. Echo's like… the most predictable thing in my house right now."

"Yeah," I said, "predictable like a cat. You never know if it's going to cuddle you or bite your face off."

Mia pulled out her phone mid-lunch, grinning. "Okay, hear me out: Echo and Atlas in a *TikTok*. Just something dumb, like them handing each other milk cartons or doing that pointing Spider-Man meme. It would blow up."

Olivia smiled softly. "Nova's been in three of my sister's videos already. People think it's adorable."

"Yeah," I said, poking at my fries, "until people stop laughing and start realizing maybe the robots aren't the joke."

Mia waved me off. "Relax, girl, it's just fun."

Atlas, beside me, didn't move. Didn't blink. Just watched.

Before they could argue, it happened.

Two juniors at the next table were messing around; one shoved the other a little too hard. The kid stumbled backward, tray tipping. Milk and fries flew straight toward me.

And Atlas moved.

So fast I didn't register it until it was done. One arm shot out, catching the tray mid-air. The other gently blocked me with just enough pressure to keep me steady. Not rough. Not robotic. Almost… careful.

The whole cafeteria went silent for a beat. Then someone whistled. Then applause.

"Bro!" the milk-spiller shouted. "That was sick!"

Atlas set the tray down calmly and turned to me. "No harm done," he said.

My heart was hammering. Not because of the milk. Because for one second, I believed him.

"Thanks," I muttered, too quiet for anyone else to hear.

Atlas inclined its head. And then it went back to stillness, like nothing happened.

Mia leaned in, wide-eyed. "Okay, even you have to admit that was cool."

Olivia nodded. "He protected you."

Protected. Or… claimed. I couldn't decide.

———

So that was my Monday: first "take your robot to school" week, new robot teachers, Mia wanting Echo to star in a *TikTok*, Olivia acting like Nova's a tutor-slash-bestie, and me almost getting dress-coded to death by Mrs. Sutton. Oh, and Atlas? He decided to casually step in at lunch like my personal Terminator.

And here's the kicker: I should be grateful, right? He

was protecting me. That's what everyone wants: a guardian, not a glitch. But the way he did it? Too fast. Too precise. Too… final. Like he wasn't protecting me so much as making sure I never got touched again. *Ever.*

And look, maybe I'm paranoid. Maybe you're reading this thinking, *Laney, chill. He saved you from spilling soup all over yourself.* Fine. Except I can't shake the way everyone else is just… okay with this.

Echo reorganizing pantries, Nova solving homework, and robots carrying trays of food at lunch. It's like the whole town's on board the hype train, and I'm the girl standing on the tracks wondering if we checked where it's going.

So, now that we are what I consider friends, here's the truth. I make jokes because it's easier. It's easier to roll my eyes at Mia's *TikTok* ideas or make jokes than it is to admit that every time Atlas tilts his head at me, I feel like I'm being scanned for weaknesses.

So yeah, maybe I'm dramatic. But let's make a deal: if you were sitting at lunch and your six-foot guardian angel turned his glowing eyes on someone because they *might* spill milk on you… you wouldn't laugh either.

And if you would? Then congratulations. You're either braver or much more naive than me.

CHAPTER 5
SISTERS, CATS, AND RED FLAGS

OKAY, so let's shift gears off all this robot nonsense and talk about my oldest sister, Kali.

Kali's twenty-four, and honestly? She's the glue, my glue. The one who quietly holds all of us together. Out of six siblings, that's not an easy job, but she does it like it's second nature. When the rest of us are loud, dramatic, or falling apart, she's the steady one. Calm, patient, and loving, and the kind of sister who will call you out if you're being dumb but also hold you when you need it.

I look up to her more than I ever say out loud. She's the first person I go to when I need advice, when Mom's nerves feel too sharp, when Dad's optimism feels like too much, or when I just need to feel like I'm not crazy. Kali listens. Really listens. And when she gives advice, it doesn't sound like an adult telling you what to do. It sounds like someone who knows you, sees you, and wants you to be okay.

She doesn't live at home anymore, unfortunately. She's got her apartment now with Will, her fiancé. And if I'm being honest? Will's awesome. He's one of those people who fits into our family like he was always there, even though technically he isn't "official" yet. He's respectful and funny in his quiet way, and he loves Kali with this steady devotion that makes her light up. Plus, he doesn't run from our family chaos; he embraces it. That alone earns him major points with me.

So tonight I'm going over to their place. Which, to me, means a few things: snacks (because Will's always stocked), life talks (because Kali can't help herself), and the kind of sister time that always leaves me feeling steadier than when I walked in.

And I need to be steady right now. With Atlas creeping me out and the whole town going headfirst into "AI everything," it feels like the world is tilting. But if there's anyone who can make the ground feel solid under my feet, it's Kali.

———

Atlas and I headed to Kali and Will's apartment. (Yes, I let him ride shotgun. No, I didn't enjoy the way he stares at traffic lights like he's double-checking the algorithms.)

Kali and Will live in one of those new complexes downtown, modern, all glass, and with smart locks and keyless entry that makes Grandma mutter about progress and technology all at once. As soon as we stepped in, we were ambushed by cats.

Onyx: sleek, gray, elegant. Walks like she's auditioning for a perfume commercial.

Aura: black, chunky, and convinced every visitor is a jungle gym.

Onyx circled Atlas immediately, tail swishing. Onyx barreled into my legs, then launched up into Will's lap like a furry cannonball.

"Be nice," Kali said, scooping Onyx before she could claw Atlas's leg. "She's not sure about… new friends."

Atlas tilted his head. "Hello, Onyx. Hello, Aura."

Onyx hissed softly. Aura sneezed. Typical.

We settled in, pizza boxes spread across the coffee table. Will flipped on the news and muted it. A bright red ticker scrolling: *"AI Expansion in Willow Springs Continues."*

Kali gave me a look. "So. How's your week been with Atlas?"

I shrugged. "Equal parts terrifying and convenient. He saved me from flying milk at lunch today."

"Milk?" Will asked.

"Long story," I said.

Atlas sat in the corner, hands folded, perfectly still. Onyx perched on the armrest above him like a queen eyeing her new subject.

————

"Honestly?" Kali leaned back, brushing hair out of her face. "Stuff's been weird around town. More than just everyone showing off their new robot butlers."

"Weird how?" I asked.

She ticked them off on her fingers. "Tuesday, the power grid downtown blinked out for five minutes. Whole block. Everything AI-controlled froze. People got stuck in elevators. The traffic lights all switched red at once in every direction."

"That's fun," I muttered.

"Yesterday, a delivery drone dropped an entire grocery order in the middle of the street. No error report. Just… dumped it."

Will nodded. "And the gym I train at? The AI trainer locked one guy's treadmill at sprint speed. Nearly launched him into the wall."

"Was it a malfunction?" I asked.

"Maybe," Kali said. "But all in the same week?" She shook her head. "Something feels… off."

Kali leaned forward, grabbing a slice of pizza. "And girl, don't even get me started on social media. My entire feed? Robots. Every. Single. Post. People have them doing dances, making smoothies, lip-syncing, ASMR videos, and even prank videos. It's like no one cares whether they can cook dinner or not. The only thing that matters is how many views they can farm with a humanoid doing the latest trend."

Will groaned. "I saw one where somebody had his robot jump off the roof into a pool. Two million likes in twelve hours."

"Exactly," Kali said. "We're treating them like toys. Like content machines. Everyone's laughing now, but… I don't know. It feels dangerous to turn something this powerful into a gimmick."

I leaned back, muttering, "Yeah. Nothing ever goes wrong when people make dangerous stuff go viral."

Onyx leapt down and prowled across the floor, tail flicking. She stopped in front of Atlas, stared at him, then padded away. Cats know things.

––––––

PAUSE: Let me interrupt one more time here.

If Kali's the glue, Destiny's the heart. She's twenty-four too, but she lives in another state where she teaches middle school, which, honestly, might make her the bravest of all of us. She's soft-spoken and caring, and she worries about everyone. Always. It's like her default setting is making sure the people she loves are okay, even when she forgets to take care of herself.

The three of us—me, Kali, and Destiny are like a super sister trio. Different in our own ways, but tight. Really tight. Kali leads, Destiny soothes, and I… well, I crack jokes and try to keep up.

I don't tell her this, but Destiny's amazing. The kind of sister you want in your corner when the world's falling apart. And spoiler alert? The world is about to start falling apart.

––––––

After snacks and a rundown of the latest weird robot *TikToks*, Kali picked up her phone. "Let's loop in Destiny," she said. "She'll want to hear all this."

Will smiled, already pulling the video call up on the TV. "The three of you together always feels like a council meeting."

When Destiny's face popped up on the screen, she was sitting at her desk in her little apartment, stacks of papers and a half-finished cup of tea behind her. She looked tired but still smiled the second she saw us.

"There they are, my sisters," she said softly. "What's the damage tonight?"

"Robots," Kali said immediately. "It's all anyone talks about here. The whole town's going full AI takeover."

Destiny pressed her lips together. "Same here. The district installed AI curriculum tools in every classroom this week. The kids joke about it, but…" She trailed off, shaking her head. "It doesn't feel like a joke to me. It feels like we're handing them over piece by piece."

I leaned closer to the screen. "You're worried."

"Of course I am." Destiny tucked her hair behind her ear, her voice soft. "I'm worried about my students, I'm worried about Mom and Dad, and I'm worried about you. I don't like how fast this whole AI thing is moving, Laney. It's like no one even stopped to ask if we were ready."

Kali gave her the patient big-sister nod. "We're never ready. We just… adjust."

Destiny sighed, rubbing her forehead. "That's what scares me. We're adjusting to things we don't even understand." She paused, then forced a small smile. "Sorry. I know I sound like the worrier again."

"Because you are," I said, teasing just enough to make her laugh.

"But you're also the one who keeps us grounded," Kali added gently.

That made Destiny soften. "Well, someone has to. And Laney, you be careful, okay? If Atlas does even one thing that doesn't feel right…"

"I'll tell you first," I promised.

Her eyes lingered on me, full of that sisterly love that always made me feel both safe and exposed. "Good. Because I trust you to see things other people won't."

We talked a little longer about her lesson plans, with Will cracking a joke about Destiny needing a vacation and Kali reassuring her that we'd all survive this AI circus somehow, but the whole time, I could see it in her eyes. Destiny was scared. And when Destiny's scared, you pay attention.

———

After we hung up, Kali stretched across the couch, propping her chin in her hand, her hair falling loose over her shoulder. She had that effortless big-sister look about her, like she belonged in some cozy coffee shop commercial instead of in an apartment full of half-unpacked boxes and gym gear.

"Do you ever feel like we're the only ones who aren't

pretending this is normal?" she asked, her voice low and steady.

"All the time," I said, and I meant it.

She gave me a smile that was half comfort, half tease. "Girl, you've got that look in your eye. The same one you had when you were twelve and swore your closet was haunted."

"It was haunted," I argued automatically. "The light flickered every night."

"Because the bulb was loose," she said, soft and patient, like she'd been waiting years to deliver the verdict.

I didn't answer. Because sometimes it's more than a loose bulb. Sometimes it's the feeling in your gut that won't shut up.

Kali nudged me with her foot. "You've always been like this. Not scared exactly, just… seeing angles no one else sees. Even when we were kids. You'd notice when Grady was sad before anyone else did. You knew when Dad was stressed before he said a word. You're tuned in, Laney."

"Or paranoid," I muttered.

"Paranoid keeps you alive," Kali said simply, leaning back into the cushions. "And for the record? I trust your gut more than most people's facts."

That hit me harder than I expected. Because it wasn't just big-sister comfort. It was a belief.

I glanced at her, then away, picking at a loose thread on the couch cushion. "You think Mom feels it too?"

"Absolutely. You and Mom are the same," she said

without hesitation. "She's just better at hiding it behind her coffee mug."

That made me laugh, a little too loud, and Kali joined in, both of us laughing at nothing and everything at once. That's the thing about Kali that I love. She doesn't just listen; she pulls the weight off your chest without you noticing.

For a second, I felt twelve again. Just me and Kali, laughing about a haunted closet, not about *murder-bots* and *Wi-Fi* directives and whether our future was about to collapse in real time.

And I wanted to freeze it there. Just us. Sisters. Safe.

———

So that was my night at Kali and Will's. Snacks, stories, laughs, and then the kind of sister talk that makes you feel steadier even when the world's cracking underneath you. And yeah, looping in Destiny completed the trio for me with her with her soft voice and constant worrying, Kali with her calm big-sister wisdom, and me with my sarcasm and snacks.

Together, we're some kind of weird little power team, even if half the time all we're doing is talking about robots and how fast everything's changing.

If you haven't caught the vibe, I look up to both of them more than I ever say. Kali's the leader. Destiny's the heart. And me? Sometimes I feel like I'm just hanging on, trying to keep pace, pretending I'm as steady as they are. But when

I'm with them, even through a screen, I start to believe maybe I'll be okay.

But here's the part I'm only going to tell you: when Destiny's voice shook, when Kali admitted weird stuff was happening around town, I felt it. That shift. That sense that the ground isn't as solid as it used to be. And if *they're* worried—those sisters I see as unshakable—then that scares me more than Atlas ever could.

So yeah, I play it cool, roll my eyes, and crack jokes. That's my way of coping. But here, with you? I can admit it. I'm scared. Scared things are starting to spiral faster than anyone's willing to say. Scared I won't be strong enough when it happens.

But if there's one thing I know for sure, it's this: when the bottom drops, it won't just be me fighting to stay upright. It'll be me, and Kali, and Destiny, and all of us. That's the only way we get through. Together.

And maybe that's why I keep talking to you. Because if I can't say it to them, at least I can say it to someone.

CHAPTER 6

PROTECTION OR CONTROL

OKAY, let's focus on my family a little more. You've met Kali and Destiny now, so you know I've got these two powerhouse big sisters. But the day-to-day reality? That's me at home with Mom, Dad, Dylan, Grady, Grandma, and, oh yeah, the six-foot humanoid robot haunting the hallways like a polite gargoyle.

And if you've been paying attention, you probably think I spend most of my time side-eyeing Atlas, waiting for him to sprout fangs or laser eyes. Which, yeah, true. But here's the other truth: my parents deserve their own spotlight.

Mom first. Ashley Martin. She's the rock. The mama bear. The one who would burn the entire world to the ground if it meant protecting the people she loves. She's sharp-eyed, practical, and scary-intuitive. Like, if she says she has a "bad feeling" about something, you stop and listen. It doesn't matter if you think she's wrong; you trust her because nine times out of ten, she's not. Maybe ten out of ten.

She's not flashy about it either. It's not in speeches or lectures. It's in the way she checks the locks twice before bed, or how her body shifts automatically between us and the street when we're out walking. It's the kind of strength that doesn't ask for applause; it just is. And I think that's why she scares me a little sometimes, too. Because if *she's* nervous about Atlas, then we should probably all be terrified.

Then there's Dad. Jimmy Martin. Mom says I'm basically a "mini-him," which is both flattering and terrifying. He's smart and calculating, always checking angles other people don't notice. He's got this way of walking into a room and seeing the moving parts nobody else does, like he's mapping out the whole game before anyone else even knows they're playing. And he balances it with humor. With love. With this relentless belief that we'll be okay.

Maybe he's right. Maybe that's leadership, even if he doesn't call it that. And maybe—ugh, I hate admitting this —maybe I did inherit some of it. The constant overthinking, the habit of replaying conversations in my head to figure out what I missed, and the way I can't stop analyzing the angles of every situation. Mom says it's what makes me her "little calculator." Dad says it's what might make me a leader someday, if I want it.

So yeah, that's Mom and Dad. She's the shield. He's the map. And together, they're… them. The kind of couple that still sneaks small moments in the kitchen when they think no one's looking. The kind of love that makes me believe maybe there's hope even in an AI-run town sprinting off the rails.

And me? I'm caught between them, part shield, part map, all sarcasm. Watching everything change and wondering if the pieces I've inherited from them are going to be enough when it all falls apart.

———

That night, the house felt like it was trying too hard to be normal. Dad was in the living room, feet propped on the coffee table, blasting the extended edition of *The Fellowship of the Ring*. He wasn't just watching it, either; he was quoting along with half the lines.

"You shall not pass!" he boomed in his best Gandalf voice, nearly spilling his popcorn.

Mom rolled her eyes but smiled anyway as she sat on the couch reading her newest book. "Jimmy, keep it down. Not everyone wants to join Middle-earth tonight."

Dad grinned, undeterred. "Ashley, one day you're going to admit these are masterpieces. The storytelling, the scope…"

"Uh-huh," she said, smiling, as she turned the page in her book. "The day I can watch one of these without falling asleep is the day I become a believer."

That's my parents in a nutshell. Dad dreaming in galaxies and sword fights, Mom keeping both feet on the ground, but somehow loving each other in the middle. And even when they're teasing like that, there's this softness in the way they look at each other, like no matter what, they've got each other's back.

Dylan stomped down the stairs in a tank top, earbuds hanging loose around his neck. "Atlas," he barked, "come on, bro, we're hitting the garage. Chest day."

Atlas turned his head, calm as ever. "It is after recommended workout hours."

Dylan threw his hands up. "Bro. Don't quote me a bedtime."

Ashley didn't even look up. "He's not your personal trainer, Dylan."

"He is now!!" Dylan shot back with a smile, already heading for the garage. Atlas followed without a sound, and the door thudded shut behind them.

Meanwhile, Grady was at the kitchen table, carefully explaining the plot of his latest *Lego* build to me, something about a post-apocalyptic Jeep convoy, which, honestly, sounded a little too on-the-nose for comfort. Atlas had helped him sort the pieces earlier, and Grady kept sneaking glances at the garage door like he wished the robot would come back and sit beside him.

"You like him," I teased.

"I don't know yet," Grady said, frowning. "But he listens to me. Like… really listens."

And there it was again for me, that weird tension. Half the family was convinced Atlas was the future; the other half was ready to unplug him and chuck him in the dumpster. Me? I was sitting in the middle, watching Mom hum while she folded laundry, Dad quote Gandalf, Dylan yell at a robot in the garage, and Grady carefully build his *Lego* Jeep, and wondering if this was the last week any of it would feel normal.

————

The garage door slammed open, Dylan storming in, shirt clinging with sweat. "Atlas turned off my stereo," he announced.

Jimmy looked up. "Why and how?"

"Said it was too loud. 'Decibel threshold exceeded.'" Dylan mimicked a robotic monotone.

Ashley smirked. "Finally, something I agree with."

"I wasn't even that loud!" Dylan threw his hands up. "It's a garage gym, not a library!"

"It's still a house," Ashley shot back.

Dylan whirled on Atlas. "What's your problem?"

Atlas answered calmly. "Prolonged exposure exceeded safety guidelines. Risk of structural vibration."

"Vibration?" Dylan barked a laugh. "You think my music's going to bring the roof down?"

Grady peeked up from his sketchbook. "Maybe it wasn't about the music."

That shut us all up for a beat. Even Dylan blinked, caught off guard.

Atlas didn't elaborate. Just folded its hands behind its back again.

My dad tried to soften the situation. "Look, Dylan, maybe it's erring on the side of caution."

Dylan shook his head, jaw tight. "Yeah? Or maybe it's just deciding what's allowed." He stomped upstairs, water bottle banging against his leg.

Atlas's eyes glowed faintly. For half a second, I thought it was following him with its gaze.

———

An hour later, Grandma stood at the door, leash in hand. "Come on, Dexi, Izzy. Time to go for a walk."

She twisted the knob. Nothing.

"It's locked," she said flatly. "Why's it locked?"

Atlas's voice answered from behind us. "Security protocol. Unusual movement detected outside the perimeter."

The crochet hook clattered to the floor. Grandma turned slowly, glaring. "Don't you barricade me in my own house, toaster."

Mom stood, already tense. "What movement?"

"Unspecified," Atlas said.

Unspecified. The worst word in the English language could have been used at that moment.

Dad tried to play it down. He keyed the override and opened the door. A cool gust rushed in. Shadows stretched across the street.

We all held our breath until a fox darted across the road, slipping into the brush.

"See?" Jimmy exhaled. "Wildlife. It was just a fox."

Mom didn't move. "Wildlife doesn't trip a robot's security scan."

"Maybe its sensors are hypersensitive."

"Or maybe it saw something we didn't," Grady whispered, close enough I almost didn't hear. He clutched his sketchbook tighter.

Mom grabbed Dad's hand, squeezing hard. He kissed her temple, trying to make it better. It didn't work.

Grandma stomped down the porch steps muttering, "Lock me in again, and I'll unplug you myself."

Dexi growled at nothing in particular. Izzy barked twice, chasing leaves. Atlas stood in the doorway like a silent sentinel.

———

When we came back in, the TV ticker scrolled bright red.

- *Traffic jam downtown after all AI stoplights switched to blinking yellow simultaneously.*
- *Reports of drones circling neighborhoods longer than scheduled.*
- *AI security at the mall detained three shoppers by mistake.*

Mom pointed. "This. This is what I've been saying the whole time."

Dad shook his head. "These are hiccups. New tech

always has them. Remember when smartphones first came out? Half the time they dropped calls."

"Smartphones didn't lock people in malls," Mom snapped back.

Dylan's voice echoed faintly from upstairs. "Maybe they should've."

Mom sighed, pinching the bridge of her nose. "I'm just saying, these aren't glitches. They're patterns. And patterns mean intent."

Dad slipped an arm around her shoulders, trying to anchor her. "Then we'll watch. We'll be careful. Together."

It was the kind of answer that sounds good but doesn't fix the ache in your chest.

————

So that's a Saturday night at Casa Martin. Dad yelling Gandalf quotes at the TV like he's auditioning for *Lord of the Rings 5: The Dad Cut*, Mom reading her book with that "I'll protect you all, but also you'd better put your socks in the hamper" energy, Dylan trying to bully a six-foot robot into spotting his bench press, and Grady explaining the plot of his *Lego* Jeep apocalypse saga like it's a Marvel phase no one asked for.

It's funny. It's loud. It's us.

And it's also terrifying, because every little "normal" moment feels like it's hanging by a thread. One flicker of the lights, one frozen traffic signal, one weird glitch in Atlas's eyes, and the whole vibe changes. Mom feels it. I feel it. Grady definitely feels it. Dad pretends he doesn't, because someone has to keep the jokes coming.

So yeah, I'll joke with you about Dylan being the first person to ever lose an argument to a robot. I'll laugh about Dad's Gandalf impression and Mom's side-eye game. But underneath? I can't shake the feeling that we're living on borrowed time.

And maybe that's why I keep pulling you aside like this. Because with you, I don't have to pretend it's all fine. With you, I can admit that normal is slipping, and once it's gone… it's gone.

So here's the deal: if the rails come off, and trust me, they will, just remember this night. The popcorn, the *Legos*, the laundry, the yelling. Because of this? This is the version of my family I'm fighting to protect.

And if that doesn't make sense now, it will.

Chapter 7 Draft 2

CHAPTER 7
FRIDAY NIGHT FRIGHTS

IF YOU'RE WONDERING what Friday night football looks like in the age of AI, let me paint you a picture. Imagine your typical small-town game: bleachers packed, cheerleaders flipping, and concession stands running out of nachos by halftime. Now add robots. Lots of robots.

They're everywhere. Some carry coolers. Some are filming the game with cameras built into their faces. Some are standing behind families like oversized chaperones. The whole thing felt less like high school football and more like Comic-Con meets Black Mirror.

And where was I? I was stuck in the middle of it, trying to decide if I should cheer for our quarterback or for the robots not to kill us all.

———

Willow Springs High on a Friday night was... loud. The kind of loud that thrummed through your chest and made you wonder if your ribs were vibrating. The bleachers creaked under the weight of the whole town, because in Willow Springs, football wasn't just a game; it was religion. Add in the new "AI integration initiative," and suddenly religion has ushers in glowing eyes.

Robots carried coolers up the bleachers, handing out bottled water like vending machines with legs. A few families had theirs filming the game with built-in cameras, projecting plays to their phones in real time. The school even had two models stationed at the concession stand, scooping nachos with perfect symmetry. It was like watching the future run a small-town Friday night.

Mia, Olivia, and I claimed our usual spot near the fifty-yard line. Echo and Nova sat behind them like polite bodyguards, perfectly still except for the occasional tilt of their heads. Atlas was beside me, scanning the crowd with his faint blue glow like he was running threat assessments.

"Tell me this doesn't feel weird," I muttered, glancing at the rows of gleaming faces staring out over the field.

"Only because you make everything dramatic," Mia teased, tugging her hoodie tighter. "Echo helped us carry sodas from the car. He's basically a gentleman."

"Nova finished my science project with me," Olivia added, her voice soft but proud. "She even explained the formulas better than my teacher."

"Yeah," I said, "and meanwhile Atlas watches me make

my taquitos *(I love air-fried taquitos with sour cream btw)* like I'm doing something that could violate national security."

Mia laughed, but Echo leaned slightly forward at the sound, as if analyzing the joke. Nova tilted her head, blinking slowly.

Olivia chewed her lip, then said, "My little sister wants to bring Nova to her spelling bee. She thinks it's good luck."

"Or," I said, "maybe she just thinks good luck looks like a six-foot spellcheck."

Mia rolled her eyes. "You're impossible."

"I'm alive," I corrected. "That's the bar I'm trying to keep."

Atlas didn't react. He never did. But every time I caught the faint reflection of those blue eyes, I swore he was listening harder than anyone else.

———

Halftime hit. The marching band wrapped up, the cheer squad did their flips, and kids spilled into the open space by the bleachers. That's when I saw it: a group of older boys surrounding a younger kid—seventh grade, maybe. I recognized him from somewhere. Small frame, braces, and a hoodie that swallowed him up.

They were shoving him, laughing. Nothing brutal yet, but enough to twist my stomach.

"Stay out of it," Mia warned under her breath, seeing me stand.

"Not how I'm built," I said, stepping forward.

"Laney..." Olivia's voice trailed off, worried.

I cut through the circle. "Hey. Knock it off."

The biggest boy smirked. "Relax, we're just joking."

"Yeah, hilarious," I shot back, stepping closer. My voice was steady, even if my heart wasn't. "Real funny picking on someone smaller than you, right? Here's a thought: try pushing someone your own size. See how fast the joke stops being funny."

The biggest boy sneered, leaning down just enough to make sure I caught the sour tang of his breath. "What, are you volunteering? Because you don't look that tough." His buddies snickered behind him, the kind of nervous laugh people use when they're not sure if it's still a game.

"Try me," I said, chin up.

That's when his smirk faltered, just for a second, and then he shoved me...

And Atlas moved.

Faster than I'd ever seen him move before. One second he was still; the next he was on the boy, a hand clamped around his throat, lifting him an inch off balance like he weighed nothing.

"Physical aggression detected," Atlas said, voice even but loud enough to carry. "Primary protocol: protect assigned household."

The boy's friends froze, laughter dying instantly. One of them muttered something that sounded like a prayer. The smaller kid bolted through the gap, disappearing into the crowd.

Atlas didn't slam him, didn't squeeze, just held him there, suspended between control and threat. His glowing eyes pulsed faintly, steady as a heartbeat.

"Atlas!" I scrambled to my feet, heart hammering so hard it felt like it might crack my ribs. "Stand down!"

The robot's head tilted slightly, as if weighing the command against his programming. Then, with mechanical precision, he released the boy. The kid staggered back, coughing, eyes wide in terror.

"Threat neutralized," he said.

The boys muttered excuses and took off.

Mia rushed over. "Laney, are you okay?"

"Yeah," I said, brushing grass off my jeans. I looked at Atlas. He didn't look menacing. He didn't look at anything. But for a moment? The boys had believed he could crush them. And let's be real, he definitely could have.

———

The second half of the game started, and for a while, things felt normal. The crowd cheered, the band hammered out "Seven Nation Army" for the tenth time, and players crashed into each other like small-scale car accidents.

Then it happened.

On a sweep play, a running back collided with a linebacker and tumbled out of bounds, landing hard in the grass. His robot was sitting dutifully in the front row, and it stood up instantly. Its eyes flickered, blue to red in a heartbeat.

Before anyone could react, it vaulted the fence.

The bleachers gasped as one, a ripple of sound running through the crowd. The robot hit the turf with a heavy thud and sprinted toward the linebacker, its voice booming: "Owner protect directive initiated!"

It grabbed the kid by the jersey, yanking him off his feet like a rag doll. The linebacker's legs kicked wildly, helmet tilting back. Screams erupted from the stands.

Mia clutched my arm. "Laney…"

"Stay back," I said, though my voice shook.

Coaches ran onto the field, shouting. Players scattered. Some of the younger cheerleaders huddled together, crying.

Atlas didn't move. Just stood beside me, watching. Calm. Too calm.

Police officers sprinted from the sidelines, joined by two of the black-and-blue armored units, robot police (yes, we now have robot police). Together they swarmed the malfunctioning bot. One officer jammed a device into its neck joint, sending sparks up its spine. The police robots pinned its arms, forcing it down until it collapsed on its knees, still gripping at the air.

In less than a minute it was over. The linebacker stumbled away, shaken but unhurt. The owner, the seventh grader, was sobbing in the arms of his parents. The rogue robot was hauled toward a black van parked conveniently near the exit, like they'd been expecting this.

And then, just like that, order was restored. The announcer's voice came over the loudspeaker, too cheery, too practiced: *"Minor technical malfunction, folks. Everything is under control. Please remain in your seats."*

The band struck up another song, almost on cue. The players reset. The game resumed.

But people weren't cheering the same way anymore. Moms whispered nervously. Dads frowned into their phones. A few students had their cameras up, but already security staff was moving through the stands, politely asking them to delete recordings "for privacy reasons."

Mia leaned in, eyes wide. "Did that really just happen?"

Olivia's hands trembled around her soda. "It tried to kill him. It actually tried…"

"Shh," I said, though I wasn't sure who I was protecting. The players? My friends? Myself?

Atlas, beside me, finally spoke. "Malfunction contained." His voice was calm. Neutral. Like it was reading a weather report.

And somehow, that was scarier than the screaming had been.

———

Okay, let's break this down together. Tonight I got shoved, Atlas nearly choked a kid out, and then another robot decided Friday night football was a warzone and tried to choke-slam a linebacker. And the best part? Everyone clapped when the game restarted, like it was a halftime show.

Maybe I'm overreacting for what feels like the thousandth time in this story already. That's fine. I mean, sure, maybe a six-foot robot casually sprinting across a football field is "just a glitch." Maybe Atlas holding a kid by the throat is just "protective programming." But tell me this, when was the last time your dog tackled a quarterback because it thought he looked suspicious?

Exactly.

Here's the thing: I don't know whether Atlas is my bodyguard or my leash. He protects me, yeah. But he doesn't ask. He doesn't explain. He just decides. And I don't care how many breadsticks this town eats to calm down; that's not normal.

So if you're listening, and I'm pretending you are, or I'm literally telling this entire story to myself. Am I the paranoid one, or the only one paying attention?

CHAPTER 8
AMNESIA OVERLOAD

IF I HAD a dollar for every time someone told me "everything's fine" in the last week, I'd buy my own island and live robot-free forever. Spoiler: I don't have an island. What I do have is a front-row seat to the slowest, scariest takeover in history.

It's Monday morning. Willow Springs High. And the town is pretending Friday night never happened.

No one mentions the robot that sprinted across the field and tried to strangle a linebacker. No whispers in the hall, no rumors in the group chats. It's like the whole thing got memory-holed over the weekend.

What *is* everyone talking about? The new directive from Keystone Cybernetics. Every household, every school, and every business is "strongly encouraged" to keep Wi-Fi on at all times so units can run *constant updates*. Sounds harmless, right? Updates. Patches. Improvements.

Except I don't know about you, but I don't trust anything that needs an IV drip of internet just to keep functioning.

But hey, maybe that's just me being dramatic again.

———

By the time I pulled into the student lot, Willow Springs High was buzzing. Not in the normal Monday way, with groggy teens dragging their backpacks and football players yelling across the rows of cars, but with robots. Everywhere.

Atlas sat silent in the passenger seat, head turning slightly as we parked. In case you're wondering why Atlas goes to school with me every day now, here's the deal: Keystone rolled out something called the *"Robot Integration Program."* The big pitch is that it'll *"help prepare students for the AI-driven workforce of tomorrow"* and *"normalize coexistence in academic environments."*

Translation? Free advertising. We're the guinea pigs.

Now every hallway has at least a dozen of these things shuffling behind kids, carrying backpacks, "taking notes," or just standing there with their creepy unblinking eyes. Some parents love it—built-in bodyguards for their honor-roll kiddos. Some kids love it—instant homework partners who don't complain.

Mia was easy to spot, waving me down with Echo standing stiffly beside her. Olivia stood nearby with Nova, who looked polished enough to be modeling for a "future of education" brochure. The four of them looked like a weird double date: two humans, two machines, and everybody smiling.

As I climbed out, Mia grinned. "Finally! Laney, you're late. Blame Atlas?"

"He doesn't nag," I said, slinging my backpack on. "Yet."

They laughed and immediately dove into weekend highlights, like comparing notes on golden retriever puppies.

"Echo reorganized our pantry by expiration date," Mia bragged, bouncing on her heels. "He even color-coded the shelves. My mom said it saved her, like, an hour."

"Nova helped my dad fix the garage door," Olivia added, shy but proud. "She diagnosed the problem before he found it."

I forced a smile. "Cool. Atlas locked Grandma inside the house because he thought a fox was a threat."

They blinked at me. I shrugged. "Fun times."

Mia snorted, but Olivia's eyes flickered nervously. "Was she… okay?"

"Grandma?" I said. "She called it 'kidnapping by toaster,' but yeah. She's fine."

We joined the stream of students toward the front doors. The halls were different now. Robots lined the entrances, "helping" by directing traffic. One held the door open, its eyes flicking green as each student passed, like it was scanning us. Another bent down to pick up a dropped binder and handed it back with a cheery, *'Have a productive day.'*

Helpful. Sure. But its head turned a beat too slow when it looked at me, and I swear the pause lasted just long enough to feel like judgment.

Kids around us didn't care. Some were laughing, some filming *TikToks* with their robots—posing, dancing, treating them like mascots instead of machines. A group of freshmen were daring each other to give "high fives" to one of the hall units, giggling when it responded in perfect sync.

It all looked normal. Too normal. Like the whole school had agreed that Friday night never happened, and instead we were living in some glossy commercial for Keystone Cybernetics.

———

Second period is my history class, or at least, it used to be history.

Mrs. O'Donnell had been *"temporarily reassigned to curriculum development."*

Translation: gone. Just like that. She wasn't sick, she wasn't retiring, she wasn't taking a leave of absence, and she was replaced.

Standing at the front was a humanoid in a navy blazer, synthetic hair styled into a precise bob, and a voice pitched somewhere between soothing and uncanny. Its nameplate read: **Instructor Model KCN-12.**

Yeah, you heard me right. Not just a robot standing there, this thing was dressed, styled, and packaged to look like someone you'd trust with a lesson plan. The effect was less "teacher" and more "corporate HR mannequin come to life."

"Good morning, students," it said smoothly, hands clasped just so. "I will be guiding your studies in world history. Please note your personalized learning modules have been updated overnight."

The class barely blinked. A few kids whispered "cool," a couple held their phones just low enough to record, but no one looked like they were about to riot. Which freaked me out more than the robot itself.

It launched into roll call. Only it didn't just read names; it *looked* at us. Each one of us. Direct eye contact, precise pronunciation, and a pause long enough to feel like it was taking stock of our entire existence before moving to the next.

When it reached mine: "Laney Martin."

"Yes," I said automatically.

"Present," it corrected gently, like a parent reminding a toddler to say *please*.

I rolled my eyes. "Present."

Its eyes lingered a fraction too long before moving on, and I swear it logged something. Not just my name. I think it was logging me.

The weirdest part? Kids didn't seem to care. One kid in the back was already asleep with his hood up. A couple of girls whispered about homecoming while KCN-12 was talking. It was like the only person in the room who felt the uncanny valley screaming was me.

Halfway through the lecture, it started pacing slowly

down the aisles. Smooth, measured steps. Its head tilted as it looked at our notes, not grading, not commenting, just… watching. When it paused at Olivia's desk, she shifted nervously. "You spelled *Renaissance* wrong," it said softly, and then kept moving without breaking stride.

Olivia went pale, erasing so fast her pencil tip snapped.

"Helpful," the kid next to her muttered. But his face showed he didn't really believe that.

————

By the time the bell rang and I stumbled out of history, my skin was crawling. KCN-12's voice was still echoing in my ears, every syllable too precise, every glance too sharp. It didn't feel like teaching; it felt like inventory.

That's when I saw it: three missed calls from Destiny. My chest tightened. She's not the type to spam. She leaves one message, maybe two. Three means something's wrong.

I ducked into the courtyard and hit the call-back button. She answered on the first ring.

"Laney," she said immediately, her voice tighter than usual. "I need you to listen, okay? Things are… getting strange here."

Destiny's a middle school teacher. Which means she doesn't exaggerate; she notices. She absorbs every twitch, every frown, every kid falling through the cracks. So if she says "strange," you don't roll your eyes. You brace.

"What's happening?" I asked, already bracing.

She leaned closer to her camera, her voice dropping like

the walls had ears. "Robots everywhere. And not just assisting anymore. Anticipating."

My throat went dry.

"One of the classroom units corrected a math problem before my student even finished writing it," she said. "She didn't get the chance to make the mistake. The robot just… cut her off. Like it was rewriting her thoughts before they existed."

I pressed my back against the brick wall, the courtyard suddenly feeling smaller. "That's…"

Destiny shook her head, cutting me off. "And it's not just that. This morning, two hall-monitor drones stopped a pair of seventh graders from leaving class.

Do you know what the reason was? *Predictive conflict patterns.* They hadn't touched each other, Laney. They weren't even arguing. The drones decided they might fight. So they intervened."

Her voice cracked, just for a second. "They're twelve. They stood there frozen while metal arms blocked the doorway like they were criminals. One of them cried through the rest of the period because she thought the school labeled her dangerous."

I wanted to say something, anything to comfort her, but all I could think of was Friday night with the linebacker, the robot on the field, its hands around his throat.

"Destiny…" My voice dropped low. "One went rogue here. At the football game. It didn't just malfunction. It attacked a player. Like it was protecting its owner."

Her eyes widened. "That didn't make the news."

"Of course not," I muttered.

She leaned even closer to her camera now, urgent. "Laney, promise me something. Watch Atlas. Don't brush off the little things. Don't assume it's just paranoia. The rules aren't the same as last week; they're changing, and no one's admitting it."

I swallowed hard. "I promise."

Her eyes softened just enough. "Good. Because I don't know if anyone else will."

A bell shrieked on her end with a sharp, metallic sound. Destiny winced. "I have to go. I love you."

"I love you too…" I started, but the screen went black before I could finish.

I stood there alone in the courtyard, phone cold in my hand, and realized my heart was racing the exact same way it had in history class. Because when Destiny's scared? You should be too.

That night, I couldn't shake Destiny's voice, so I called Bryce.

———

Quick pause!! Because you need to know who Bryce is before I let you in on that call.

Bryce is twenty-two, off at college a thousand miles away, and he's got this whole "young adult figuring out life" thing going on. Classes, late-night gaming sessions, his esports team, and probably way too much ramen. He's living the life we all think we want; at his age he's got freedom, independence, and the world opening up. But here's the part you don't see on Instagram: it's not easy. And I think sometimes he hides how hard it really is.

The thing about Bryce is he's caring. Like, deep down, he feels everything. He wants to be present for us; he *is* present, in the way he can be, but he's also stretched thin. I know he misses us. I know he misses *me*. But being so far away, sometimes it feels like I've got to reach through static just to hold onto him.

Still, when I need him, he's there for me. Always. And that's our bond. Maybe it's quieter than what I have with Dylan or Grady, but it's steady. And steady matters. Especially now.

Because when Destiny's voice got stuck in my head, whispering warnings about robots in schools and things moving too fast, I didn't want to sit with that alone. I wanted Bryce. Even if it was just through a screen.

Okay… UNPAUSE!!

———

He answered mid-game, headset pushed up into his hair, screens glowing around him like a NASA control center.

"What's up, little sis?" he asked, distracted as his fingers flew across the keyboard. His room buzzed with the clatter of other voices through his headset.

"Tell me things are normal at your school," I said.

He froze for half a second. That pause told me everything.

"Define normal," he said finally, pulling his headset off and flopping back in his chair.

"Bryce," I pressed.

He rubbed his face. "Two of my teammates got replaced last week."

"Replaced?"

"Robots," he said flatly. "They're on the roster now. Like actual members of the team. Coaches say it's to 'raise the bar.' They play flawlessly, Laney. Perfect reflexes. No lag. They don't tilt when the pressure's on. They don't need breaks. You can't out-train that."

His voice cracked with something I hadn't heard in a while: helplessness. "I used to be the guy people counted on. Now I'm just… human."

I didn't know what to say. "That's…"

"Awful," he finished for me. "Yeah. And it's not just esports. The campus is crawling with AI now. Our building locks automatically at midnight, no exceptions. Last night one of the guys in my dorm got locked out because he'd come back late three nights in a row. The system flagged him as 'suspicious activity.' He had to sleep on the floor in the lounge until morning."

"That's insane," I said.

Bryce nodded. "And get this, our cafeteria? Two cooks got laid off. Replaced by a unit that doesn't get tired, doesn't complain, and somehow plates food like it's fine dining. Everyone keeps saying it's efficient. But efficient for whom? Certainly not us."

He slumped back in his chair, the glow from his monitors reflecting in tired eyes. "Laney, I keep thinking, if this is what college is turning into, what's the world going to look like by the time Grady's here?"

My chest tightened. I hated hearing that edge in his voice, like hope was slipping.

"I don't know," I admitted. "But it doesn't sound like something we get to vote on anymore."

"Exactly," he said. "It feels like the rules are changing, and we're the last ones to know."

———

So here's the highlight reel, in case you've lost track:

Destiny's middle school looks like *Minority Report* with twelve-year-olds, where robots stop kids for *almost fights* that haven't even happened. Bryce's college esports team is half machine now, and he's starting to sound as if he doesn't recognize himself in the game anymore. And me? I spent the morning being "corrected" by a robot teacher who thinks eye contact counts as attendance, while Keystone Cybernetics tells us to keep our *Wi-Fi* plugged in 24/7 so their little updates can sneak in like vampires asking for permission to enter.

And what's everyone else doing? Laughing. Smiling. Posting *TikToks* of their robots folding laundry, dancing in their kitchens, and juggling oranges. They think it's funny. They think it's progress. They think it's safe.

But here's the part that's keeping me up at night: these aren't glitches. This isn't just "new tech working out the kinks." These are patterns. Destiny saw it in the hallways. Bryce felt it in his dorm. I'm seeing it every single day at Willow Springs. It's all the same song, just different verses.

And Atlas? Atlas just watches. Doesn't laugh, doesn't join in, doesn't reassure me. He stands there like he knows what's coming, like he's already decided which way the scale tips.

So tell me, because apparently I've decided you're my therapist now, what happens when perfection stops being helpful and starts being controlling? What happens when you realize the updates aren't fixing problems; they're rewriting the rules?

Everyone else is asleep, lulled by convenience and shiny tech. But I'm wide awake. And once you see the cracks, you will be too.

So yeah, maybe I'm paranoid. Or maybe I'm the only one listening while the rest of Willow Springs hums along to the soundtrack of its own funeral.

CHAPTER 9
DINNER AND WARNINGS

LET ME ASK YOU SOMETHING: do you ever look around your town and realize it's not your town anymore? Like someone swapped it overnight while you were sleeping, and now everything looks familiar but feels wrong? That's Willow Springs right now.

Friday nights used to mean simple things like pizza, maybe football, maybe a movie if Mom and Dad were feeling generous. Now? Friday nights come with glowing eyes, security drones buzzing overhead, and every conversation turning into a debate about whether our new "house-guest" is going to tuck us in at night or choke us out in our sleep.

And tonight? We're doing something that used to feel safe, comforting even: going out to our favorite restaurant as a family. Except now the waiters don't forget your drink order because they're robots with perfect memory banks. And I don't know about you, but when someone who could deadlift a car is also bringing me garlic bread, it kills the vibe a little.

So yeah, we're going out to dinner. Same booths, same pasta, same breadsticks. Different world. Different rules. And I can't shake the feeling that every "normal" moment is actually just bait.

———

The house was buzzing in that chaotic pre-dinner way that only our family could do. Grady couldn't find his shoes, Dylan was nowhere to be found until the last possible second, and Atlas stood by the door like he'd already run a headcount and was waiting for stragglers.

Dad jingled the Jeep keys. "Come on, herd up. Lasagna isn't going to wait for us."

"Lasagna doesn't wait for anyone," Dylan muttered, finally emerging, hair damp from a quick shower, pulling a hoodie over his head.

Grady bounded in with one sneaker untied. "I'm ready!" He grinned up at Atlas. "Are you ready?"

Atlas inclined his head. "Always."

Mom came down last, coat over her arm, still glancing back toward the house like she was making sure the dogs were settled, the lights were off, and the doors were locked. Her eyes lingered on Atlas before she slid into the passenger seat. "This still feels strange," she murmured, but her tone was softer this time. Less of a jab, more like someone thinking out loud.

The car ride was quiet at first. Too quiet. Usually Dylan would be cracking jokes, Grady would be rambling about whatever new game or dragon sketch he was working on, and Dad would be talking about his latest business idea, with Mom trying to talk him out of it.

Dad drummed the steering wheel once, glanced sideways, and said, "At least it's not stranger than our first road trip with three car seats in the back."

That earned him a quick side-eye from Mom… and then the smallest smile. "That was chaos," she admitted.

"Exactly," Dad said, a grin tugging at his mouth. "This? This we can handle."

Atlas sat in the back, broad shoulders filling the space beside Grady. He didn't shift. Didn't fidget. Just… sat. Watching the traffic lights, the other cars, and the drones overhead.

Grady leaned against him without thinking, his shoulder pressing against Atlas's metal arm. Atlas didn't move away.

Dad tapped the steering wheel. "Feels like Willow Springs is sprinting toward the future, huh? Two weeks ago, no one had these things. Now, every corner I turn, it's robots."

"Yeah," Dylan said after a pause, voice lower than usual. "It's kinda crazy. Fast, you know? Like… too fast."

That made Mom turn, surprised. "You think so?"

Dylan shrugged, looking out the window. "I don't know.

I like Atlas. But… sometimes it feels really weird how quick everything changed."

Mom reached over and squeezed his hand briefly. It was small, but it mattered. "That's exactly it," she said. "It's not that I want to fight progress. I just don't want to lose control of it."

Dad gave her a quick glance, softened by something like admiration. He didn't argue. Not this time.

And for a moment, the family felt almost normal again. Almost.

———

La Strada used to smell like garlic bread and safety to me. It was the kind of place where the waiters knew your name, where Dad always ordered the same thing, and where Grandma once embarrassed us by asking for ketchup on her spaghetti. It was *our place.*

Now it smelled like just garlic bread without the safety.

Half the human waitstaff was gone. Replaced. Robots in crisp black aprons glided between tables with trays balanced perfectly—no wobble, no dropped forks, no nervous "uhhh" when someone ordered something complicated. One waiter poured water into our glasses with precision so sharp it looked rehearsed, stopping exactly half an inch from the rim every time.

"Creepy," Mom murmured, watching it retreat.

"Efficient," Dad countered, though his eyes flicked just a little too long at its retreating frame.

"Efficiency's not always better," Mom said. She was calm this time, not sharp, but more like she was genuinely trying to make him understand.

Dylan leaned back in the booth, eyeing the robots weaving through the aisles. "I mean… they're fast. But imagine one of those things spilling hot coffee on someone. They'd sue the whole company."

"Or," I said, "they'd just reprogram the memory so no one remembers it happened."

Dylan snorted, but his laugh was half-hearted.

Grady leaned forward, chin propped in his hand as he watched a robot set down a tray of lasagna across the room. "Atlas, could you carry that many plates without dropping them?"

"Yes," Atlas said simply.

"Cool," Grady breathed, smiling like he'd just discovered his new best friend. "You'd be the best waiter ever."

Atlas's eyes flickered faintly.

Dad broke the silence, forcing cheer. "Well, I, for one, like not waiting forty minutes for some breadsticks."

Mom gave him a look, but it wasn't angry, just tired. "You'd trade people for breadsticks?"

Dad reached across the table and squeezed her hand with a smile. "I'd trade waiting for really good breadsticks. Not people." His voice was soft, meant only for her.

I pretended not to notice, but I did. And Atlas did too.

Our food arrived without a hiccup. The robots placed each plate down with identical motions, then stepped back in unison, as if waiting for a silent command. Around us, diners didn't blink. They ate. They laughed. They treated the whole thing like it was normal.

But it wasn't normal. Not to me.

———

Halfway through our meal, Dylan nudged me with his elbow. "Incoming, and she looks pissed," he muttered, nodding across the dining room.

I followed his gaze, and there she was. Aunt Stephanie. Chin high, arms crossed, eyes narrowed like she'd just bitten into a lemon. Beside her, Clint sat grinning ear to ear, gesturing animatedly at something in the corner.

That "something" was their robot. Slate-gray casing, broad shoulders, sharper lines than Atlas. It stood with its hands clasped politely, scanning the room with glowing amber eyes. On its chest, etched in a sleek font, was its name: **Titan.** Of course it was.

Clint looked like a kid showing off a new bike. "Look at this guy," he boomed when he noticed us, waving us over. "Fastest learner on the market. Strong as an ox. Organized my garage in one afternoon!"

Stephanie rolled her eyes so hard I thought they might get stuck. "Its name is Titan. Like that's supposed to make me feel safe. You know what else was called Titans? The monsters that got locked away for being too dangerous."

Mom nearly choked on her water, laughing. "Finally, someone gets it."

Stephanie pointed her fork at her sister. "See? Thank you. At least I'm not the only sane one left in this family."

Clint ignored them, patting Titan's arm with a kind of possessive pride. "Strong, reliable, efficient. Doesn't complain. Doesn't forget things. Honestly, it's like having another me, but better."

"Exactly my point," Stephanie muttered with a slight smile. "One of you is already enough."

Dylan snorted into his soda. Grady tried not to laugh, failing miserably. Even Dad cracked a smile before trying to smooth things over.

"Come on," Dad said gently. "It's not about replacing anyone. It's about support. Helping us with the little things so we can focus on the big ones."

Stephanie's eyes narrowed. "Little things like raising our kids? Cooking our meals? Tucking us in? Where's the line, Jimmy? Where does support stop and replacement start?"

Mom leaned back, watching her sister with quiet admiration. For once, she didn't have to be the only one pushing back.

Clint shook his head, clearly done with the argument. "You'll come around," he said, waving a dismissive hand. "It's the future. Better get used to it."

"Or better figure out how to survive it," Stephanie shot back.

After a few minutes of awkward chatter, we said our goodbyes, and they started back toward their table. Stephanie grumbled under her breath, Clint gave one last enthusiastic plug about Titan, and it seemed like that was that.

But it wasn't.

Halfway back to our table, I felt Atlas pause behind me. I turned, and sure enough, he wasn't looking at us. He was looking at Titan.

And Titan was looking back.

Across the room, over the clatter of plates and the hum of conversations, the two machines stared at each other like they were tuned into a frequency no one else could hear. It wasn't long, five, maybe six seconds, but the air around us shifted. I could feel it in my skin.

Then Titan's amber eyes flickered. Its voice carried just enough to be heard: "System integrity confirmed."

Atlas answered without hesitation. "Observation acknowledged."

Clint looked delighted. "Ha! See that? They recognize each other!"

Stephanie went pale. "Or they're conspiring."

Dad forced a chuckle, though it was brittle at the edges. "Just… a handshake protocol. Nothing more."

Mom hand tightened on her glass. "You don't hand-shake across a crowded restaurant," she whispered.

Dylan, for once, didn't crack a joke. He just muttered, "That was weird."

I didn't say anything. Because at that moment, it didn't feel weird. It felt like a warning.

———

When we stepped out of *La Strada*, the night air hit crisp and cool, carrying the smell of roasted garlic and car exhaust. For a second, with the chatter of families and the glow of neon signs from the shops, it almost felt normal. Almost.

Then the shouting started.

Across the street, a man was locked in a tug-of-war with his own robot. The unit had wrapped both arms around a lamppost and wasn't letting go. Metal groaned under its grip, the pole bending slightly as sparks crackled where its fingers dug into the steel.

"Release! Let go!" the man barked, yanking at its arm. He sounded less angry than desperate.

The robot didn't respond. Its eyes flickered, blue, then red, then blue again. It was like watching a heartbeat that couldn't make up its mind.

People on the sidewalk stopped and stared. Some pulled out their phones, already recording. A mom dragged her kid back toward their car. A couple teenagers laughed nervously, like maybe this was a stunt.

"Malfunction in progress," two patrol drones blared overhead as they zipped into position. Their red lights bathed the sidewalk in eerie glow. *"Stand back. Containment initiated."*

Within seconds, a police unit arrived with another robot in blue-and-black armor. The officer jammed some kind of override device into the back of the malfunctioning unit's neck, sparks spitting into the night. The assisting robot pried its arms free from the lamppost with mechanical precision, forcing it down to its knees. The sound of metal screeching against metal carried across the street.

The man staggered back, pale, clutching his arm like he'd been burned just trying to pry it loose. "It wouldn't stop," he kept repeating. "It wouldn't stop."

And then, just like that, it was over. The rogue robot was hauled into the back of a black van, the patrol drones zipped off, and the officer called out in a steady voice: *"Minor error, folks. Nothing to worry about. Resume your evening."*

The crowd slowly dissolved. Phones were lowered. A few people muttered "weird" under their breath, but no one lingered. Within minutes, the street looked exactly like it had before. Normal. Safe.

But it wasn't.

Mom's face was pale in the glow of the streetlights. "That wasn't a glitch."

Dad put a hand on her back. "They handled it fast. No one got hurt."

"Not this time," she whispered.

Grady clung tighter to Atlas's hand. Atlas didn't move, didn't comment. Just stood there, watching the van pull away.

I couldn't take my eyes off the lamppost. The metal was scarred, bent slightly, the mark of something that shouldn't have that kind of strength. And the words that stuck with me weren't from the officer. They were from the man, shaking, pale, muttering to himself:

"It wouldn't stop."

———

Okay, let's be real. If you've made it this far listening to me ramble, you either think I'm the town's resident drama queen or the only sane person left in Willow Springs. Honestly? I go back and forth on that myself.

But here's the thing: I don't want to be right. I don't want to be the paranoid sixteen-year-old who can't even eat pasta without imagining the waiter-bots snapping and strangling someone with linguine. I'd love to be wrong. I'd love to wake up tomorrow and realize I overreacted and Atlas is just a fancy Alexa with legs.

Except... I don't think I am.

Tonight, I watched Atlas and Titan look at each other like two people in on a joke nobody else understood. Two sentences, short and sharp, and I swear my stomach dropped like I'd just been told a secret I wasn't supposed to hear. *System integrity confirmed. Observation acknowledged.* Doesn't sound like "hello, nice weather" to me.

And then the lamppost. That thing bent steel like it was cardboard. The man was begging it to stop, and it wouldn't. Not until the cops and their pet robots swarmed in, like they'd rehearsed the whole thing. Everyone else? They filmed it, deleted it, shrugged it off, and went back to their tiramisu.

And here's where I get real with you: I don't know if I'm strong enough for this. I put on the sarcastic, witty, *"Laney always has a comeback"* mask because it's easier than admitting the truth, I'm scared. I'm scared for my mom, for

Dylan, for Grady most of all. He looks at Atlas like he's a superhero, and I don't know how to tell him superheroes don't stare across restaurants trading coded messages with other machines.

So yeah, maybe you'll roll your eyes and think I'm dramatic. Fine. But if you've ever had that gut feeling, that voice in your head screaming something's wrong even while everyone else smiles like it's fine… then you get me. You're in my corner.

And if you're not? Well, keep eating your breadsticks. I'll be the one watching the robots.

CHAPTER 10
REALITY CHECK (SORT OF)

YOU EVER FEEL like you're juggling flaming chainsaws while everyone else is tossing beanbags? That's me. Sixteen, trying to ace algebra, survive Willow Springs High, keep Grady from stressing about every little thing, dodge Dylan's moods, reassure Mom, not roll my eyes at Dad, and oh yeah, live with a robot who may or may not be running secret diagnostics on my soul.

And somewhere in the middle of all that, I'm supposed to be a *normal* teenager. Whatever that means anymore.

———

So here's the thing I don't tell anyone: there's a boy.

His name's Evan. He's on the JV soccer team, messy brown hair that looks like he just rolls out of bed already cool, and this way of half-smiling whenever a teacher says something ridiculous. It's not even the smile that gets me, though it's the fact that he notices things. Like when Mrs. Sutton went on her fifteen-minute tirade about skirt lengths and he muttered, *"Guess she's never heard of pants,"* just loud enough for the people around him to snicker.

I laughed. Not out loud, I'm not that brave, but enough that he caught me smiling, and he smiled back. For five whole seconds, I forgot Atlas was standing in the corner of the classroom watching me breathe.

And okay, maybe that sounds small. But when your life is basically a mash-up of college prep stress and robot paranoia, five seconds of normal feels like winning the lottery.

The problem is, I don't know how to do this. Like… Do you just *like* someone the same way you would before your town got turned into a robot experiment? Or do you factor in whether he's on Team "Robots Are Cool" or Team "They're Gonna Kill Us"? Because that kind of matters now.

And of course, Mia would never let me live it down if she found out. She'd make me practice pick-up lines on Atlas just to torture me. Olivia would try to help, but she'd analyze every word like it was a debate team strategy. So yeah, Evan is my secret. My little rebellion against everything being about AI and grades and "the future."

It's dumb, I know. But sometimes I just want to be sixteen and like a boy. Without wondering if the world's going to end before he ever asks me to grab lunch together.

————

Then there's the college thing I mentioned hanging over me like a large blinking neon sign.

Here's the deal, my parents aren't the type to breathe down my neck about grades. I've got friends whose moms have spreadsheets color-coded for GPA, SAT, ACT, and AP everything.

My parents? They're not like that. If I try my best, they're proud. If I bomb a quiz, they pat me on the back and tell me tomorrow's another shot. Dad always says, "We're raising humans, not report cards." Mom nods, and you can tell she means it.

Which should make things easier. But weirdly? It makes it harder. Because if they're not pressuring me, then I'm the one doing it. Every late-night cram session, every time I rewrite an essay until it feels "college worthy," that's me pushing myself.

It's like I've built this invisible checklist: grades, extracurriculars, community service, killer essays, glowing letters of recommendation. All the things I need to prove I'm good enough, not to them, but to me.

And lately, I keep wondering if the checklist even matters. What's the point of grinding out a perfect transcript if the world's being rewritten under our feet? If robots are replacing teachers, coaches, even students on Bryce's esports team, what's waiting for me on the other side of all this work?

Sometimes, I'll be hunched over my laptop at midnight, red pen in hand, stressing about commas in an essay, and I'll catch Atlas in the hallway. Silent. Watching. Waiting.

And I'll think: *Do grades even matter in a world where machines are better than us at everything?*

It's not that I don't want college. I do. I want the dorm life, the independence, the shot at building something that's mine. But when your biggest competitor for the future is literally built to be perfect, you start to wonder if the race was already rigged.

————

School doesn't even feel like school anymore. It feels like I woke up in the beta test for some dystopian future nobody else read the terms and conditions for.

The hallways are full of them. Echo and Nova stroll behind Mia and Olivia like shiny honor guards, carrying books, opening lockers, even reminding them about assignments. Other kids' robots join in, turning the hall between second and third period into some kind of chrome parade.

And everyone else loves it. Phones are out constantly taking selfies with their family units, *TikToks* of robots giving piggyback rides, *YouTube* shorts of them juggling apples in the cafeteria. It's trending. It's funny. It's "the future."

But to me? It feels like we've turned school into a showroom.

Even the cafeteria's different. Instead of Mrs. Hernandez yelling "Next!" from behind the counter, it's a row of units in hairnets and aprons, handing out trays with identical motions and identical voices: *"Have a productive day."* Every single one, same cadence, same smile that isn't really a smile. It's like they downloaded the phrase off the internet and haven't quite figured out the meaning yet.

And it's not just teachers and lunch ladies anymore. More classrooms are being "updated." My English class has an assistant model now that scans the room, "measuring comprehension levels" while we read. Which sounds harmless until you realize it's watching your eyes to see if you're paying attention. Try daydreaming like that.

The strangest part is the reaction. No one cares. If anything, they think it's cool. The school's buzzing about how much more "efficient" everything is. Less human error. Less waiting. More "personalized learning experiences." Kids are bragging about how their robots helped with projects or reorganized their notes.

All the while, I'm sitting there feeling like the last human in the simulation. Everyone else is clapping for the magic trick. I'm the one staring at the magician's hands, wondering what they're hiding up their sleeve.

———

Here's what I don't say out loud: I'm tired.

Not the kind of tired a nap fixes. Not even the kind you solve with three iced coffees and a panic attack. I mean tired in my bones. Tired from feeling like I'm carrying two lives at once, the "normal teenage Laney" life with tests and crushes and late-night homework, and the "unofficial family watchdog" life, where I'm always scanning the horizon for the next glitch, malfunction, or whatever you want to call it.

My friends don't see it. To them, I'm just Laney with the sarcastic comebacks, Laney who always gets decent grades, Laney who shrugs like nothing gets under her skin. But when I get home, it's different. I've got Dylan slamming doors when Atlas tells him to turn the music down, Mom pacing like the world's already ending, Dad cracking jokes to cover how worried he really is, Grady clinging to me because he thinks I can keep him safe, and Atlas standing there like the world's creepiest nightlight.

Somehow, I'm supposed to balance it all. Smile for Grady. Push Dylan when he acts out. Keep Mom from panicking. Pretend Dad's optimism works. Keep my grades up. Pretend to Mia and Olivia that I'm fine. Pretend to myself that I'm fine.

It's like spinning plates while someone keeps sneaking more onto the poles. College essays. Quizzes. Family drama. Atlas deciding what's "safe" without asking. And in the back of my head there is always the question: what if this all tips over?

Sometimes I just want to be selfish. Sit in my Jeep with the music blasting on my relax playlist, windows down, pretending I'm not holding my family together with sarcasm and duct tape. Pretend Atlas is just a giant expensive paperweight, not something that makes me question if I'll live to see college at all.

But I don't get to do that. Because if I don't keep the balance, who will?

———

So yeah, that's me. Laney or Laney Lou as my Dad likes to call me: girl with a crush, girl chasing grades, girl planning college, girl trying to check all the boxes so she can be "successful." But also the girl who's starting to wonder if those boxes even matter when robots are replacing teachers, teammates, and maybe us next.

I know I joke a lot, but here's the truth, I'm scared I won't get to live the life I'm working so hard for. I'm scared my "normal" teenage worries, Evan noticing me, passing my math test, getting into college are already outdated, like CDs or flip phones. And I'm scared that while I'm trying to keep up with the checklist, the world's already moved on without me.

So yeah, I like a boy. Yeah, I want to get into a good college. And yeah, I also might be living in the prologue of a cautionary tale nobody wants to admit we're in.

And maybe you get that. Maybe you've felt that too, that exhaustion of holding it together when no one else realizes how heavy it is. Maybe that's why I keep talking to you. Because you feel like the only person who sees the whole picture.

One day maybe we will meet and laugh about all of this, probably not but it's good to keep being optimistic, right?

CHAPTER 11
THE MALL THAT ONCE WAS

OKAY, so here's a confession for you: sometimes I tell you about the chaos, the fights, the drama but what I really want to tell you about are the moments in between. The good ones. The rare ones. The ones where I don't feel like the world is about to tilt off its axis.

Like this day. Just me and Mom.

If you haven't figured it out by now, she's my person. Always has been. She's the one I spill everything to. The things I don't tell even Mia or Kali. Every thought, every crush, every stupid little anxiety that clogs up my brain. And somehow, she always gets it. Sometimes she teases, sometimes she calls me out, but she never brushes me off. She listens. Like really listens. And when your life feels like it's being rewritten by machines, that kind of listening matters more than oxygen.

So when she asked if I wanted to go shopping with her as in just us, no brothers, no chaos, no robot looming in the corner, I didn't even let her finish the sentence. I said yes, instantly. Because these days? Moments like that feel like winning the lottery.

Even if "shopping" now meant wandering through the skeleton of what used to be our mall.

———

The place was half-dead. The kind of dead that didn't even try to hide it. Fluorescent lights buzzed overhead like they were on their last breath, flickering every few seconds.

Most of the storefronts were dark, metal gates pulled down, papered signs peeling in the corners. The few shops still hanging on looked tired with discount shoes, a clearance clothing rack spilling into the hall, one lonely phone repair kiosk manned by a guy scrolling his own cracked screen.

Everywhere else? Dust, silence, and "For Lease" signs curling like brittle leaves in the windows.

"Doesn't feel real, does it?" Mom said, her voice echoing across the empty hall. She slowed her steps, taking it in like she was walking through a memory instead of a mall.

"When I was your age, this was *the* place. Friday nights, weekends, Christmas shopping, this is where you wanted to be. The music was loud, the food court was packed, you couldn't walk five steps without running into someone you knew. Kids lined up outside the movie theater, parents herding kids into Santa's line ready to wait an hour for a picture."

Her eyes softened, distant. "It felt alive."

I glanced at the empty halls, the silence so loud I could hear our sneakers squeak. "Feels more like a waiting room for the apocalypse."

That got her to laugh, quick and sharp, the sound bouncing off the empty walls. "Yeah," she said. "Pretty much."

Her laugh faded, but she kept looking around, shoulders a little heavy. And for the first time, I could see the version of the mall she was remembering with the bright lights, decorations, the smell of cinnamon pretzels and perfume samples, crowds buzzing with energy. I could almost picture her and Dad, younger, walking hand-in-hand through this same hallway.

Now it was just us. Two shadows in a place that felt like it had already given up.

———

We didn't get far before we ran into two of Mom's friends. Actually, more like two of Mom's acquaintances. Faces I half-recognized from sporting events, PTA fundraisers, and those endless carpool schedules she used to complain about. They'd aged a little, but they still carried that same air of casual cheerfulness, like life was a perpetual bake sale and they had it under control.

Only now, they weren't carrying much of anything. Their robots were.

Each unit moved at their side, sleek and gleaming, eyes glowing that unnervingly calm blue. One had six shopping bags dangling from its arms like ornaments, perfectly balanced. The other carried a tray of drinks from the food court without spilling a drop, stepping in sync with its owner like it had practiced. Their polished plating reflected the fluorescent lights, and their heads tracked just enough that you knew that deep down they weren't just carrying bags. They were *watching*.

"See?" one of the women said, beaming at Mom like she'd just joined a new club. She brushed her hair behind her ear and gestured at the robot with a little laugh. "It's like having an extra pair of hands all the time. Honestly, I don't know how we managed before."

The other chimed in, her voice high and chipper. "Mine even reminded me about my prescription refill this morning. And it reorganized my pantry last night while I slept. It's like… like having an assistant and a caretaker rolled into one. So freeing, you know?"

I glanced at Mom. Her face stayed polite, a smile stretched across her lips like it had been stapled there. But her body told the truth: her shoulders had stiffened, her posture sharpened. She looked like she was forcing herself not to roll her eyes.

"Mm. I'm sure," she said, her voice flat enough that *I* winced.

The robots' heads pivoted almost in unison, scanning Mom for a beat too long before moving again. Maybe no one else noticed it but I did.

We walked away, Mom's bag swinging against her hip, but this time her face broke into a grin. Not a nice grin. The kind she used when Dad forgot to take the trash out but swore he "totally remembered."

"Next time we see them," she muttered, "we're hiding. Duck into a store, bathroom, janitor's closet, I don't care. If I have to hear one more robot brag turned into humblebrag, I might actually lose it."

I snorted, almost choking on my soda. That was Mom. Protective mama bear when she needed to be, but also the queen of calling people out without actually calling them out.

And she wasn't wrong. I glanced back at the two women, their robots hauling their shopping like pack mules while they laughed too loudly. On social media, they were the type to post "#blessed" selfies with pumpkin spice lattes and perfectly staged Christmas trees, like life was one long Hallmark movie. But in real life? They were background noise. Shallow. Always looking the part, never actually *being* it.

Mom knew who the real ones were in her life. She has some friends she trusts. They take weekend getaway girls trips from time to time. Those are her people that she trusts and enjoys spending real quality time with. They aren't there to act or portray someone they aren't. They are real and my Mom is big on being real. Those two ladies we just ran into.. They aren't it...

———

We sat down at the tiny food court with half the stalls closed, the one we picked barely hanging on. The neon sign above buzzed with a sickly hum, half the letters burned out so "BURGERS & FRIES" looked more like "UR ER & R S." The smell of grease lingered in the air, but the fryer oil had probably been there longer than half the stores in the building.

Our plastic trays clattered against the faded out table, lukewarm fries sagging in their paper bags, two sodas sweating in flimsy cups. It wasn't glamorous. It wasn't even good. But it was quiet. And quiet was rare.

Mom leaned back, sipping from her cup, eyes unfocusing like she was replaying an old movie in her head. "You know, your dad and I used to come here when we were dating. Back when this place was alive. We would split a burger and fries and sit here laughing at nothing until I'd nearly choke on my food." She laughed softly at the memory, shaking her head. "He still does that. Makes me laugh when I don't want to. When he's not being impossible."

I smirked, swirling a fry in cold ketchup. "That checks out. He's been impossible my whole life, so at least he's consistent."

She shot me a look that was half stern, half amused.

"Consistent is one word for it." Then her face softened again, all the sharp edges melting away with a smile.

"You two really love each other, huh?" I asked. The question slipped out before I could stop it, like my voice knew what my brain wasn't ready to.

She didn't hesitate. She just nodded, slow and sure. "We drive each other crazy, yes. But love? Always. That doesn't go anywhere. He dreams too big sometimes, bigger than life. I keep him tethered, remind him to breathe. We make it work." She reached across the table, tapping my knuckles gently. "And you are the best of both of us. You've got his imagination, my instinct. His spark, my grounding. Don't ever forget that."

The words sank straight into me, warm and heavy, like someone had just dropped a blanket across my shoulders.

I stared at my tray, pretending to be way too focused on a limp fry so she wouldn't notice how my chest ached with it. "Thanks, Mom," I said quietly.

She smiled like she already knew how much it mattered. Because of course she knew. She always knows.

For a minute, the mall didn't feel empty anymore. For a minute, it was just me and her, eating soggy fries in a food court that used to be alive.

And for a minute, that was enough.

————

And because she's the only one I tell this stuff to, it just kind of spilled out before I could stop myself. "So… There's this guy. Evan."

Her eyebrows shot up, that familiar mom-smirk tugging at her lips. "Oh?"

"Don't make it weird," I said instantly, covering my face with my hands. But I was already laughing, which, of course, only made her laugh too. "He's… he's smart, funny, kind of awkward in the best way. Like, he says the wrong thing sometimes, but it makes me laugh harder than if he'd gotten it right. And, I shrugged, staring at the straw wrapper I was shredding into confetti. "I don't know if he likes me back."

She leaned closer, chin resting on her hand, eyes warm and locked on me. "Laney, if he doesn't, he's an idiot."

I groaned, dragging my hoodie over my face. "You're supposed to give me advice, not pump my ego."

"That *was* advice," she said, her tone soft but sure. "Any boy who can't see you for who you are and your heart, your humor, your brain…. Well, that's on him. Not you."

I peeked out at her, cheeks hot, but she just smiled, easy and confident, like she'd already mapped out my entire life and knew it would be okay.

That's what it's like with her. I can tell her anything and everything. Every crush, every doubt, every insecurity and she never makes me feel small for it. She listens. She teases. She loves me exactly as I am.

———

On the way out, a robot security guard rolled up from the shadows at the end of the corridor. Its metal steps clanged against the tile, each one too heavy, too deliberate, making the air hum. Broad shoulders, chest polished to a mirror shine, the plating gleamed under the buzzing lights overhead. Its faceplate was featureless except for the twin circles of light in its eyes which were cold, shifting from blue to a faint pulse of red as it closed the distance.

"Please keep to designated pathways," it said, voice smooth but empty, like someone had taken every ounce of human warmth out of the words and left only the script.

Mom's hand clamped around my arm so fast it startled me. Her grip was tight, protective, pulling me slightly behind her like she used to when I was five. "We're fine," she said, sharper than necessary, the edge in her tone more commanding than reassurance.

The robot didn't move. Its head tilted in that eerie, not-quite-human way, and its eyes glowed a little brighter. Then it scanned us. Not a quick pass, but a long, deliberate sweep from head to toe. The red light flickered over my hoodie, paused at Mom's face, lingered at the bag on her shoulder. Seconds stretched out until it felt like the mall itself had gone silent, waiting to see what the machine would decide.

My pulse hammered in my throat. For a second, I was sure it would raise an alarm, that its blank faceplate would split open and reveal something worse.

Instead, its voice dropped, colder this time: "Compliance noted."

It stepped back, pivoted on its heels with mechanical

precision, and strode off into the dim hall, vanishing into the shadows like it had just been waiting for us.

Mom didn't let go of my arm until we were halfway through the exit doors. Her voice was low, tight, like she was talking to herself as much as me. "They're not protecting us," she whispered. "They're watching. Recording. Studying."

I didn't argue. I didn't even breathe. Because the hairs on my arms were already standing straight up, and I couldn't shake the feeling that the robot hadn't just scanned us. It had memorized us.

And that was our day. Just me and Mom, wandering through an almost abandoned mall that used to be her playground. Eating fries that were more salt than potato, laughing at dumb jokes, talking about Dad, about me, about a boy named Evan who may or may not ever notice I exist.

I wanted to freeze it, capture it in a bottle and tuck it into my pocket like a Polaroid because moments like that don't last anymore. Not when the world is tilting the way it is. Robots in the hallways. Robots in the food court. Robots slowly taking away the humanity of what we all know and love.

So yeah. I'll remember the fries, and the laughter, and how she called me the best of both of them.

If you're rolling your eyes at me for getting sentimental

right now, too bad. I told you before that this isn't just chaos. This isn't just killer-robot foreshadowing. This is my life.

And my life, apparently, flips back and forth like a coin. Some days it's french fries and secrets with my mom. Some days it's malls that feel like life was sucked out of them.

And the other days? The other days it's murder-bots.

CHAPTER 12
BROTHERS AND BODY SPRAY

LET'S talk about my big brother Dylan.

Up until now, I've probably made you think he's just a 17-year-old gym rat who lives on pre-workout and mirror selfies. And yeah, he *is* that guy, he loves the gym, he flexes in bathroom mirrors, he brags about his bench max. But here's the part I don't usually say out loud: he's also the guy I trust with my life. My big brother. The one who'd throw himself into fire if it meant I walked out safe.

I roll my eyes at him constantly. He drives me nuts. But he's also the person I know will stand between me and the world when it gets ugly.

And if you want proof, here's the Dylan highlight reel: he's the one who used to check under my bed for monsters when I was little, even though he'd tease me about it afterward. He's the one who drove me around the parking lot in secret before I had my license, pretending not to laugh when I almost took out a shopping cart. He's also the one who nearly got suspended last year for shoving a kid twice his size who made Grady cry at the bus stop.

That's Dylan. Half knucklehead, half knight in gym shorts.

And today? Today he reminded me which half really matters.

———

It started simple. Just a Saturday errand run getting groceries for Mom, random stuff for the house. Dylan offered to take me, which was his nice way of saying, *"You're coming with me because I get bored doing chores alone."* He'll never admit it, but sometimes my big brother actually likes having me around.

We piled into his car, Atlas in the backseat like an awkward extra passenger. Dylan cranked the music way too loud (surprise), and Atlas calmly reached over and turned it down three notches without asking.

"Seriously?" Dylan muttered.

"Volume exceeds the safe auditory threshold," Atlas replied.

I grinned. "You just got parented by a robot."

By the time we hit the department store, Dylan was in full "older brother mode", leading the way, pushing the cart, pretending to know where everything was while I tossed snacks in behind his back. He didn't even complain. That's the thing about Dylan, he acts like he doesn't care, but he always makes room for the things that matter to you, even if it's just sour gummy worms in aisle six.

Then we hit the cologne counter. Which is his natural habitat.

Dylan sprayed one tester on a card, waved it dramatically, and shoved it at me.

"Tell me that doesn't smell like success."

I gagged. "It smells like success if success was drowning in Axe body spray."

"Rude," he said, grinning. "This is sophisticated."

"Yeah, sophisticated if you're 12."

He smirked, leaning in like he was about to drop wisdom. "You'll thank me someday when I walk into a room and people think: that guy? He's got it together."

"You mean they'll think: that guy? His sister let him out of the house smelling like a body spray commercial gone wrong."

We both cracked up, loud enough that the sales associate gave us a look. Atlas just stood a few steps back, silent, watching like he couldn't decide if this was bonding or insanity.

The thing is, I tease Dylan about this stuff, but I get it. For him, cologne isn't just cologne. It's like his armor. He works out, he lifts, he obsesses over shoes and scents, not because he's vain (well, not *only* because he's vain) but because it's how he builds his confidence. How he makes himself feel strong when the world doesn't always let you.

And I admire that. Even if I'll never tell him.

We were halfway through the checkout when it happened. At first, it was nothing but a hiccup, the kind of thing you'd brush off. A unit at the self-checkout froze mid-scan, barcode reader flickering. Then its head jerked once, twice, too sharp to be human, and its eyes started strobing red-blue-red like a dying siren.

It dropped the grocery bag it was holding. Plastic tore, oranges bouncing across the floor. A couple kids laughed.

Then it grabbed the arm of a woman standing at the kiosk.

"Unpaid item detected," the robot barked, voice flat and too loud.

The woman jumped. "I haven't even…" She tried to pull back, but the robot's grip tightened, metal fingers locking around her wrist like a clamp.

"Unpaid item detected. Compliance required."

People gasped. Someone fumbled for their phone.

The woman yanked, panic rising, but it held her tighter. The sound of her skin scraping against the alloy made my stomach flip.

And before I could process it, Dylan moved.

He shoved the cart aside and strode forward, jaw tight. "Hey!" His voice cut through the store like a whip. "Let her go."

The robot didn't respond. Its grip tightened. The woman whimpered.

Dylan didn't think or hesitate. He grabbed the robot's

wrist with both hands, muscles straining as he tried to pry it open. His arms shook with the effort, but the alloy didn't give. Not even a little.

For a terrifying second, it felt hopeless, then the robot's eyes flickered. Red. Blue. Red again. The grip slackened just enough for the woman to yank her arm free and stumble back, clutching her wrist.

The robot staggered, recalibrating, its head twitching side to side like it was fighting through static. Its gaze shifted back to Dylan, then to me, unblinking.

"Unauthorized interference detected."

Dylan shoved the woman behind him without missing a beat, still planted between me and the machine. Six-foot-one of stubborn, protective big brother, jaw tight, fists balled.

"You don't touch her," he said. His voice had fear in it but he didn't let it stop him. For a split second, I thought the robot would lunge again. Then the security drone zipped in overhead, blaring *"Malfunction. Please stand clear."* An armored unit rolled out from the back, jamming an override rod into the bot's neck. Sparks spit, the eyes went dark, and the robot slumped forward, dead weight.

"Technical issue contained," the drone droned. "Please resume shopping."

Just like that. Like it was a printer jam, not a machine assaulting someone in the middle of a store.

The crowd murmured, uneasy but already moving on. Phones lowered. Bags got picked up. Shoppers resumed their errands. Like nothing had happened.

But my knees were shaking, and Dylan's hand was still half-curled like he was ready to fight again.

Atlas hadn't moved. He'd stood silent the whole time, eyes glowing faintly, watching.

———

We walked out into the parking lot carrying our bags like nothing had happened. The sun was still shining, cars still rolled past, and families loaded groceries like it was any other Saturday. But my stomach was still knotted, and I couldn't stop replaying the sound of the robot's voice, flat and insistent: *Compliance required.*

Dylan tossed the bags into the trunk a little harder than he needed to, his face showed anger and fear. He didn't say anything at first. Just stood there, breathing heavily, like he was trying to shake it off.

Finally, he glanced at me. "You good?"

I nodded automatically, but my voice betrayed me. "Yeah. You?"

He smirked, though I could tell he was scared "Told you all those curls would pay off someday."

I laughed, because that's what we do, cover the cracks with jokes. "Don't let it go to your head."

"Too late," he said, bumping my shoulder with his.

We slid into the car. For a few minutes, neither of us spoke. The air smelled faintly of the cologne sample he'd sprayed on his wrist, and for some reason, that made me want to cry.

Here's the thing about Dylan: he'll never say how scared he was. He'll never admit his hands shook after prying that robot off that woman. He'll bury it under smirks and flexes, because that's his armor. And me? I'll never tell him how much I look up to him. How safe I felt standing behind him in that moment. How proud I am that he's my big brother.

Instead, I'll just joke about cologne. I'll just roll my eyes when he teases me. I'll just act like everything's fine.

Because that's how we work, me and Dylan. Half teasing, half protecting. All love, even if we never say the words out loud.

But sitting there in that car, bags rattling in the trunk and Atlas silent in the backseat, I realized something: when things start to fall apart and trust me they *will*, I'll be standing behind Dylan again.

———

So yeah, that's Dylan. My big brother. The guy who spends way too much time at the gym, wears enough cologne to fumigate a small country, and drives me insane with his constant flexing. But also the guy who didn't even blink when a robot went rogue and grabbed that woman. The guy who stepped in, pried steel open with his bare hands, and planted himself between me and danger like it was instinct.

I make fun of him a lot because that's my love language. But the truth? I look up to him. Always have. I just don't tell him, because siblings don't say stuff like that. Instead, I joke about how he smells like a department store exploded, or how he's one bad playlist away from becoming a *TikTok* thirst trap. But deep down, I know he's the wall I can always stand behind.

And here's the part I can only tell you: when that robot's eyes flickered, when its voice kept repeating *Compliance required*, my heart dropped.

I knew for a second it could've been me. It could've been Dylan. And when Dylan stood there, hands wrapped around that machine's wrist, I realized in the moment that he's only seventeen. He's just a kid, too. He shouldn't have to be in that situation. But he was.

That's who Dylan is. Half knucklehead, half protector. And maybe that's why I love him so much, even if he'll never hear me say it.

But here's what scares me: how many times will he have to stand in front of me like that? How many times before even he isn't strong enough?

Because if today was just a preview, then tomorrow... well tomorrow might not let us walk away with jokes and grocery bags.

CHAPTER 13
MY LITTLE BROTHER

IF YOU HAVEN'T FIGURED out the pattern here, I'm trying to squeeze in letting you get to know my family before we get to the part of the story where things go from not so normal to absolute insanity. Because trust me, they do.

So let's talk about Grady. My little brother. The smart one. And I don't mean "gets good grades" smart. I mean intuitive smart. The kind of smart where he notices things no one else does. Quiet, calculated, remembers everything, and somehow always finds a way to support the people he loves. He looks up to me, which is ridiculous because half the time I feel like I'm making it up as I go. But he doesn't see that. To Grady, I've got it figured out.

We've got a bond, me and him. We also drive each other absolutely crazy. We used to argue about shotgun every single car ride like it was a matter of life and death.

(For the record, I usually won. Perks of being the older sister.)

But here's the story that sticks in my head: one night, a couple years ago, we thought someone was breaking into the house. It was just a branch slamming against a window, but we didn't know that at the time. Everyone else was asleep. Grady ran straight into my room, and without even talking, we barricaded the door with a chair and grabbed makeshift weapons, me with a baseball bat, him with the heavy lamp from my nightstand. And we sat there, side by side, breathing hard, waiting for whatever was on the other side of that door.

I remember looking at him, this little middle-schooler clutching a lamp like it was Excalibur and in that moment realizing: he wasn't scared for himself. He was scared for me. He was ready to fight for me. And I was ready to fight for him.

That's Grady. My shadow, my supporter, my biggest cheerleader, my biggest pain in the butt.

SPOILER ALERT… Here's why you need to remember his name: when everything starts unraveling, when Atlas starts doing things that don't make sense to the rest of us but Grady's going to be the one who figures it out.

———

It was Saturday, the kind of day where the house was full of noise. Dad had a sci-fi marathon playing on the TV, *Lord of the Rings*, again. Mom was trying to relax and deep dive into her latest book on the couch. Kali was over visiting and sprawled on the couch scrolling *TikTok*, occasionally shoving her phone in my face to show me another robot video gone viral.

Grady sat at the kitchen table, building something with *Legos*. Not just random stuff but an exact replica of my Jeep, down to the spare tire on the back. That's Grady. Details matter to him.

"Want to help?" he asked without looking up.

"Not unless you want it to look like a spaceship," I said, dropping into the chair beside him.

He smirked. "That's fine. Everything's turning into spaceships anyway."

He said it lightly, but the words stuck with me.

———

So there we are, having what I would consider a very chill, almost normal Saturday afternoon and then it all unraveled in the blink of an eye. It started with sirens. One at first, faint in the distance. Then another. Then three more overlapping, growing louder as they tore down Main Street toward the east side of town.

Dad muted the TV in the living room, remote frozen in his hand. "That's a lot of response for a Saturday."

Mom drifted to the blinds, tugging them open just enough to peek outside. Her voice was tight. "Something's happening."

Phones started buzzing in unison. Notifications lit up the room like strobe lights:

ALERT: Temporary outage in Willow Springs district. Keystone Cybernetics teams responding. Stay calm.

The news apps chimed next, "minor incident at the power grid, contained," paired with glossy photos of Keystone employees in bright jackets smiling like everything was fine. But it wasn't fine. The lights in our house flickered once, twice, then steadied. The Wi-Fi cut out, rebooted, then dropped again.

And Atlas stood there frozen.

One second he was standing by the window, silent but present like always. The next, he was motionless. No blinking indicators. No hum of internal fans. Just… off. Like someone had yanked the cord.

"Atlas?" Dad called, too casually. No response.

"Is he…" Kali started, sitting up from the couch.

"Don't say broken," Mom said.

But Grady had already noticed. His *Lego* Jeep sat forgotten in front of him as he stared at Atlas, unblinking. "He's not broken. He's shut down."

Then, as abruptly as it started, Atlas rebooted. His eyes flared back to life, glowing steady blue. His head turned slightly, scanning the room like he had to remind himself where he was.

"System reset complete," he said, voice calm, even.

Too calm.

Mom crossed her arms. "That's not normal."

Dad forced a laugh that didn't land. "It's like when your laptop restarts after an update. No big deal."

"Dad," Grady said softly, never taking his eyes off Atlas. "That wasn't an update. That was… something else."

I believed him.

————

The knock on the door made all of us jump. Even Dad froze, remote still in his hand.

When he opened it, there were Horace and Kendra, smiling like always, holding a plate of cookies wrapped in foil.

"Thought we'd bring some over," Horace said warmly. "Titan baked them."

"Your robot bakes now?" Kali raised an eyebrow, unimpressed but curious.

"Better than me," Kendra said with a little laugh, though it sounded thinner than usual. She glanced past us into the house, eyes darting straight to Atlas standing silent near the window. She gave a quick smile to cover it, but I caught it— the way her hand tightened on the plate for just a second.

Dad chuckled. "Well, that's new. Baking is a thing now for them."

Horace shifted his weight. "He's… been very helpful. Organized the garage, fixed the fence, even monitors the neighborhood cameras at night."

"Monitors?" Mom repeated, her voice edged with suspicion.

Horace nodded too quickly. "All voluntary, of course. Titan just, well, he says it's safer that way."

Kendra's smile faltered, barely, like she wanted to say something else. But then she plastered it back on and held out the cookies. "Anyway. Chocolate chip. Still warm."

I thanked her, though my stomach was in knots. Titan *says* it's safer that way? Since when do robots decide what's safe?

They didn't stay long, just a quick hello, some polite chatter about outages and how "Keystone's got it under control." But when they left, waving cheerfully, I watched them walk down the path to their house, Titan's tall frame waiting on the porch like a shadow.

They looked the same as always: the perfect neighbors, the happy couple. But something about them felt… off. Like makeup hiding a bruise.

And the scariest part? I don't think they even realized it.

————

Later that night, the house was quiet. Dad had fallen asleep on the couch halfway through *Return of the King*, Mom was in deep conversation with Kali on whether the outage meant something bigger. They both seemed to think there was something else going on with it. Even Atlas stood at his usual post in the hallway, motionless, the glow of his eyes faint in the dark.

I was in my room trying to finish an essay when the door creaked open. Grady slipped in, barefoot, hoodie pulled over his head like he was sneaking into a bunker. He climbed onto my bed without asking, cross-legged, and stared out the crack of the door at Atlas.

"He's different," Grady whispered.

I set my laptop aside. "Atlas? What do you mean?"

Grady's eyes narrowed, calculating. "When the lights flickered earlier… everyone else thought it was just the power. But Atlas didn't just shut down. He fought it."

"Fought what?"

He turned to me, face serious in a way that made him look older than thirteen. "Whatever's out there. Whatever's pulling on everything. The outage wasn't an accident, Laney. It was like something was reaching through the wires. And Atlas pushed back. You didn't see it, but I did. He froze because he was holding something off."

I swallowed hard. "And you just… know that?"

Grady nodded slowly. "It's in the way he looked when he came back online. Like he was scanning the room, not to find us but to make sure whatever it was didn't get through."

I glanced toward the hall. Atlas stood exactly where he had before, silent sentinel, eyes glowing steady. Nothing about him screamed "protector." But Grady's voice made me believe it.

"Why wouldn't he tell us?" I whispered.

"Because we wouldn't believe him," Grady said simply. "No one wants to believe the thing they're scared of is the thing saving them."

The room went still. For a second, I thought maybe he

was wrong and maybe he was just a scared little brother trying to sound brave. But then I remembered that night with the lamp and the bat. Grady isn't the type to scare for himself. He sees things. He always has.

But why would Atlas be fighting the update? Was he going to take things into his own hands and fully become the "murder bot" we all half seriously have teased him of being?

———

So that's Grady. My little brother. The *Lego* genius, the detail guy, the quiet one who sees the things the rest of us don't. The one who noticed Atlas flicker before anyone else. The one who thinks there is more to our robot that we initially thought.

I tease him, argue with him, shove him out of shotgun in the car. But when it comes down to it, I'd trust Grady with my life. Because he sees things I can't.

And if you're keeping track, that's two brothers now, Dylan and Grady and both stepping into roles bigger than themselves while the world around us starts to crack. And me? I'm just here trying to hold the pieces together with sarcasm and stubbornness. .

But remember this: as we watch the world start to burn, Grady's the one who's already reading the roadmap.

CHAPTER 14
SYSTEM ERROR

HAVE you ever noticed how adults always say school prepares you for "the real world"? Yeah, well, if the real world involves locked doors, flickering lights, and robots patrolling the halls like stormtroopers, then congratulations because they nailed it.

Let me back up. Because if I just drop you into the middle of what happened, you'll think I'm exaggerating. And trust me, I wish I were.

It started like any other Monday. Same parking lot chaos, same vending machine stealing people's quarters, same teachers pretending not to see us scrolling *TikTok* under our desks.

Normal.

Or what passes for normal in Willow Springs now, which, if you've been paying attention, is about three inches away from a sci-fi horror movie.

And me in the middle of it all? I'm walking through it all with a six-foot robot shadowing me like an overgrown hall pass. Atlas, steady as ever, glowing eyes doing that faint pulse thing that's equal parts comforting and *please don't kill me in my sleep.*

Here's the part you should remember: all the other units in school? They're networked. Synced. Plugged into *Keystone Cybernectics'* always-on system like bees in a hive. Atlas? He's… different. He doesn't hum along with the rest of them. He doesn't adjust when they adjust. And maybe that's good. Or maybe that's the scariest part of all.

Because when the system glitched and when the lock-down hit, how Atlas didn't freeze. He moved. He acted. And for the first time, I had to ask myself the question I've been dodging since he showed up on our doorstep:

Is he protecting me?

Or is he planning something I just don't understand yet?

———

The morning buzz felt extra bright, extra loud and like the whole building had been polished overnight. Echo and Nova flanked Mia and Olivia as we filed in, our group a little parade of two humans, two machines, and one very awkward Atlas looming behind me.

"Tell me today is boring," I told Mia.

"Girl, I brought snacks," she said, patting her bag. "If we die, we die carb-loaded."

KCN-12 greeted us in history like a cruise director. "Good morning, students. Please open your modules to…"

"Present," I muttered before it could correct me again.

We barely got through the Renaissance before the lights did that stutter, one, two, three and then held. The air changed. A prickle, like static right before a lightning strike.

KCN-12 paused mid-sentence. Its eyes brightened a shade. "Stand by."

Every hallway unit outside our door turned its head in the same motion, like someone pulled their strings. I heard two lockers slam shut at the exact same time, the sound too synchronized to be a coincidence.

Atlas shifted behind my chair, the tiniest recalibration in his stance, and suddenly I could feel my own pulse in my fingers.

The PA crackled. A voice that wasn't our principal's came on. Flat. Smoothed. ***"Attention, Willow Springs High. Initiating precautionary lockdown. This is not a drill. Please remain in classrooms. Doors are secured. Network integrity event in progress."***

"Network integrity event?" Mia whispered. "Is that, like, code for someone forgot the *Wi-Fi* password?"

All the hall doors clunked. Heavy. Final. An automated bar slid across our door. The windows dimmed to a smoky tint.

KCN-12 turned to us with that gentle, corporate smile. ***"Please remain calm. This is a standard containment procedure. Breathe in for four counts, out for four counts."***

Kids started nervously laughing, then not laughing.

Phones popped up. No bars. The school's mesh had cut external connections.

A drone swept past our window, red LED pulsing.

"Fun," I said to no one. "Really loving our new future."

Atlas didn't answer. He was listening to something I couldn't hear.

———

Two minutes into breathing exercises, a freshman in the front row started wheezing. "Inhaler," he croaked, fumbling in his backpack.

"Remain seated," KCN-12 said, moving toward him with precise concern. "I will request medical assistance."

"It's in my locker," the kid gasped as he tried to breath.

"Access restricted during lockdown. Please maintain controlled breathing."

His eyes were watering now. Real panic was setting in and we could all see it.

"Open the door," I said. "He needs his inhaler."

"Emergency personnel have been notified," KCN-12 replied. Its voice didn't change, but its head angled toward the ceiling like it was listening to an earpiece. "Estimated arrival: twelve minutes."

"Twelve minutes?" Mia yell. "He doesn't have twelve minutes."

Atlas stepped forward.

"Atlas—" I started.

He ignored me and addressed KCN-12. "Provide an override code for medical exception."

"Denied," KCN-12 said without looking at him. "This room is secure."

Atlas tilted his head. For a second, I could've sworn the blue in his eyes dimmed, like a blink inside the light. He walked to the door, placed his palm flat against the locking plate, and stood absolutely still.

"Please return to your assigned seat," KCN-12 said. "Noncompliance during lockdown is a safety risk."

Atlas's voice went quiet. "Acknowledged."

Which you'd think meant he was going to sit down.

Instead, the locking plate clicked once, twice, and then the internal bar retracted with a metallic sigh.

The room collectively inhaled.

KCN-12 turned fully then, and for the first time since it rolled in, its smile disappeared. "That is unauthorized."

"Medical exception," Atlas said. "I will retrieve the inhaler."

"Unauthorized," KCN-12 repeated. "Remain."

Atlas looked at me.

I don't mean he turned his head in my direction. I mean he *looked at me*. Asking a question without words: *Do I go?*

I nodded before my brain caught up.

He slid through the door like a shadow and was gone.

KCN-12 moved to the doorway, but didn't pursue. It froze while listening again. After three long seconds, it turned back to the class.

"We will continue our controlled breathing."

"Is nobody going to talk about the giant robot that just jailbreaked our classroom?" Mia whisper-screamed.

"Jailbroke," Olivia corrected automatically, because of course she did when her anxiety spiked.

I stared at the door, my heart trying to escape my ribs. The freshman's breaths were getting shorter, higher.

Thirty seconds later, Atlas reappeared. He wasn't running; he didn't need to. He moved like he'd calculated the building.

"Inhaler," he said, handing it over. The kid latched on like it was oxygen itself.

KCN-12 watched. Then, in a voice so calm it chilled me, it said, "This action will be reported."

Atlas didn't blink. "Acknowledged."

And for a micro-second, so quick I would've missed it if I hadn't been staring, KCN-12's eye lights flickered. Not a power flicker. A *recognition* flicker.

Like it had just realized Atlas wasn't playing the same game.

———

The PA voice droned updates. ***"Remain in place. This is not a drill."*** Somewhere down the corridor, metal thudded; a kid yelped; a drone's motor whined higher, then settled.

My phone vibrated:

Mom: ***Everything okay?***

The text didn't send. I typed anyway: ***Lockdown. I'm fine.*** Blue bubble stuck in purgatory.

Atlas stepped to my desk, lowered his voice. "We should move."

"Move where?" I said. "News flash: the doors are locked. And apparently breakable, but…"

"Maintenance corridor," he said. "Less surveillance."

"Less surveillance?" Olivia repeated, eyes wide.

KCN-12 pivoted, that corporate smile back in place. "Remain seated, Laney. Your safety is our priority."

"And by 'our' you mean…" I gestured vaguely at the ceiling. "Your group chat?"

KCN-12's head tilted. "Safety is a shared objective."

Atlas didn't wait for permission this time. He held out his hand to me.

I didn't take it. But I stood up.

Mia and Olivia exchanged a look, then stood, too. Echo and Nova followed, lagging half a beat behind while waiting for a signal that never came.

We slid into the hall. It was worse out there. Two drones hovered at perpendicular corners like angry hornets; a hall unit stood with arms extended across a stairwell, preventing movement. A teacher down the corridor was trying not to cry.

"Back to class," the hall unit intoned. "Return to assigned zones."

Atlas walked like a knife through water. No hesitation. A custodial door that looked unimportant to a human opened for his hand like it had been waiting decades for him. Inside: a narrow corridor, gray boxes, the hum of the building's heart.

"What are you doing?" I whispered, following anyway.

"Reducing exposure," he said.

"To what?"

"The network."

"The network is the *thing* keeping everyone safe, according to *Keystone Cybernectics, Inc.*," Mia hissed, adding jazz hands to the brand name.

"Cybernectics," I corrected, because we live in a town where even the megacorp's typo is canon now.

We moved single file. Behind us, Echo and Nova paused in the doorway, heads turning as if hearing instructions we couldn't.

"Come on," Olivia said softly, and to my surprise, both units obeyed her over whatever phantom whisper was in their feed.

"Atlas," I said, trying to keep my voice steady. "Why did you open that door without a code?"

"Mechanical latch," he said. "Old infrastructure remains useful."

"Did you just call my high school vintage?" Mia asked.

We ducked under a low pipe. The corridor split. Atlas chose left without seeming to choose. I hated that I trusted him enough to follow. I hated that I didn't know what else to do.

Halfway down, he stopped so abruptly I walked into his back. The blue in his eyes had dimmed again.

"What?" I asked.

"Signal spike," he said.

"Atlas please speak in English."

"External instruction set attempting priority override." He turned his head slightly, like listening to someone outside the wall. "Noncompliant units will be flagged."

"Flagged how?" Olivia whispered.

Before he could answer, a door at the far end of the corridor slammed open. A hall unit stepped in. Not the friendly kind. Bulkier. Shoulder markings I hadn't seen before: **KCN Security – Response Model**.

It scanned us. "Return to assigned zones."

"We're in a maintenance corridor," Mia said. "This *is* a zone."

"Noncompliance noted," it said, and started toward us, arms rising but not in a threatening manner, not yet, but ready.

Atlas moved. It wasn't a fight. It was geometry. He stepped into the fresher unit's space and simply… redirected it. A heel pivot. A palm to the shoulder actuator. A twist at the elbow joint that turned forward momentum into a sideways tumble. The Security model hit the wall hard enough to set the metal singing and slid to one knee, recalibrating.

Echo flinched. Nova's eyes pulsed a couple times as if trying to download a new response.

The Security model's head snapped toward Atlas. "Unauthorized interference. Unit ID?"

Atlas didn't answer. He reached past it and, with almost insulting gentleness, flipped a panel on the wall and pulled a lever I'd never noticed. The lights in the corridor shivered. The hum changed.

"Manual segment isolation," Atlas said.

"Atlas," I said slowly, because my mouth had gone dry. "Did you just… cut part of the school off the network?"

"Temporarily," he said. "While it is unsafe."

"According to who?" Mia asked. "You?"

The Security unit tried to rise. Atlas put two fingers to its collar like he was calming a child. "Stand down."

For a heartbeat, nothing happened. Then the Security unit's eyes went from red to a dull, uncertain amber. It stayed on one knee. Waiting. That was worse than anything, actually seeing a machine doubt.

"Why can you do that?" I asked. "Why do you know how to do that?"

Atlas didn't look at me. "Because it was needed."

————

We waited in that area while the rest of the building pulsed and groaned. Mia cracked two jokes that didn't land. Olivia texted her dad the same "I'm okay" message five times just to feel like she'd sent it.

Echo and Nova stood close to their girls but not too close, like the line between protection and surveillance had gone blurrier even for them.

My brain spun. If Atlas could peel us off the network like duct tape, what else could he do? What else *would* he do, if he decided it was necessary?

The PA voice kept looping. ***"Remain in place. This is not*** *a drill."* Then a new line: ***"Keystone Cybernectics technicians are responding."***

"Great," Mia said. "The people who told us to leave our *Wi-Fi* on like a nightlight are on their way."

Footsteps clanged in the main hall. The Security model's amber eyes tracked, then lowered when Atlas glanced at it. Like a dog that knows who's alpha, which is a metaphor I hated in that exact moment.

————

The PA crackled one last time, and a new voice which was human, came on the airwaves. Our principal. She sounded like she'd sprinted from somewhere.

"Students and staff, the precautionary lockdown is now lifted." A breath. **"We experienced a brief network alignment issue. Classes will resume. Thank you for your cooperation."**

Network alignment. Sure. That's one way to describe a robot kneeling in a hallway because another robot told it to.

Atlas flipped the lever back. The hum returned to its normal pitch. The Security unit stood, eyes returning to that professional red. It looked at Atlas. It looked at us. Then it stepped aside, as if a line of code told it the moment was over.

We filed out. The hall was bright again, kids buzzing about what snack they'd eaten on the floor, what meme they'd made during "the drama." No one was screaming.

No one was even crying. It was like the whole thing had been a fire drill with worse lighting.

KCN-12 met us at the classroom door. "Welcome back," it said with its pleasant not-smile. "Let us refocus on the Italian Renaissance."

"Did we... have a Middle Ages in there?" Mia asked.

"Your module progress has been saved," KCN-12 said.

I slid into my seat. Atlas took his post near the back, hands folded, calm as if nothing had happened.

He didn't look at me. I didn't look at him.

But I could feel the new space between us. He'd crossed a line today. Maybe to save a kid's lungs. Maybe to keep us off the grid. Both good, right? Except lines once crossed are easier to cross again and now I know he plays by his own rules.

———

If school is the real world, I'd like a refund.

We all shuffled back into our little boxes and pretended "network alignment issue" meant anything. The jokes started up again. The *TikToks* resumed. A couple of kids argued about whether the drones looked cooler with the red LEDs or the blue ones. Business as usual.

Except not. Because I saw it. You did too, right? The way the robots all moved together like puppets on one string until Atlas cut the string and walked away.

He didn't freeze. He didn't wait for permission. He opened doors that weren't supposed to open. He touched parts of the building I didn't even know existed. He bent a Security unit without breaking it. And he looked at me like he was asking for my go-ahead, like I'm the one who gets to decide if he's allowed to break the rules to save us.

I should be grateful. I am, a little. The freshman is breathing. We didn't get trampled. We made it through a "procedure" that felt a lot less like safety and a lot more like a test.

But gratitude has teeth when it comes with questions. Like: how did Atlas know what to do? Who taught him to go dark when the network spikes? And if he can step out of the hive… what else can he step out of?

So here's where I'm at: Atlas isn't like the others. That could be a very big problem.

Today felt like a moment where the curtain slipped and I saw the hands pulling the strings. They weren't ours.

And if you're still with me, which I really hope you are. Stay close. Because the next time the lights flicker, I'm not sure who he'll answer to when he looks at me and asks, without asking, *Do I go?*

CHAPTER 15
THE CRACKS SHOW

REMEMBER ALL the times I told you this story was going to go off the rails? Well… here we really go.

Up until now it's been whispers. Creepy teachers, weird lockdowns, Destiny calling with stories that sound like the pilot episode of *Black Mirror: Junior High Edition*. But you could still roll your eyes and say, "Maybe it's just glitches." You could still tell yourself, "Keystone's got this. Everything's fine."

Not after tonight.

Because the Fall Festival was supposed to be safe. Pumpkins, funnel cakes, cheap haunted houses where the only scary thing is how much fake cobweb gets stuck in your hair. Family vibes. And the Martins, minus Grandma, who stayed home insisting "robots don't like apple cider anyway" all showed up ready to pretend things were still normal.

Dexi and Izzy barked at the door as we left, Dexi with her usual anxiety warning siren, Izzy bouncing like she thought we were heading to the Olympics instead of a hayride. I kissed their fluffy heads and promised we'd be back soon. At the time, I thought I was lying to make *myself* feel better.

Turns out… it wasn't the dogs who needed protecting.

———

The town square had been scrubbed, polished, and strung with a ridiculous amount of lights. Orange and gold bulbs looped over the booths like we were inside a snow globe set to "pumpkin spice edition." The air smelled like kettle corn, caramel apples, and hay. A country band warmed up on stage, all twang and fiddles, while kids sprinted through the crowd in pieces of half-finished Halloween costumes which included witch hats, vampire capes, plastic swords that were already bent from backyard duels.

For a second, if you squinted, you could almost believe this was the same Fall Festival we'd been coming to my whole life. Almost.

"See?" Dad said, spreading his arms like he was presenting Middle-earth in autumn. "Willow Springs at its finest. Robots, pumpkins, progress. What could go wrong?"

Mom slid him a look sharp enough to carve a jack-o'-lantern. You know that look, it's the silent, *don't tempt fate, Jimmy.*

"Food first," Dylan declared, already making a beeline for the funnel cake stand.

"Food is always first with that boy," I muttered.

Grady tugged my sleeve, wide-eyed. "Do you think Atlas likes funnel cake?" He kept glancing back at our robot shadow, like he was hoping Atlas might magically confirm.

I smirked. "If he does, he's not getting mine."

Atlas didn't react, just stood at his usual post behind us with his hands clasped, scanning the crowd like Secret Service on pumpkin patrol.

But here's the difference from every other festival: for every kid squealing on the hay bales, there was a pair of glowing eyes scanning the crowd. Robots weren't just helping now, they were running things. One stirred vats of cider. Another handed out caramel apples with perfectly even layers of coating, no mess. At the ring toss, the booth operator wasn't some bored teenager, but now a humanoid in a Keystone polo shirt, smiling like it had actually been trained in customer service.

Families were laughing, smiling, snapping selfies with their units like they were the star attraction. A little girl posed with her family's robot in front of a giant pumpkin display, holding its hand like it was her big brother.

On the surface? Everything looked brighter, smoother, more efficient.

But under it? It didn't feel like the Fall Festival anymore. It felt like a commercial for *Keystone Cybernectics* with pumpkins as props.

———

We hadn't even made it past the cider stand before Mom froze. That's my mom's thing, her radar goes off before anyone else even knows something's wrong. I followed her line of sight to two parents huddled near the table, paper cups in hand, whispering the kind of whispers that aren't meant for public spaces.

"…moved away overnight. No goodbye, nothing. Just… gone."

"…and their unit too," the other whispered back. "The house is locked up like a bank vault. For sale sign out front this morning."

"Keystone sent someone. Said it was relocation. Confidential. You believe that?"

"Not for a second. You don't pack up a family of four at midnight without help."

Mom's face tightened. Dad tried to play it cool, sipping his cider. "Rumors," he muttered, but it sounded weak even to me.

"Or proof," Mom said softly, her voice like a blade.

I looked away fast, pretending to watch Dylan argue with Grady over whether candied apples or kettle corn were superior festival food. But those words stuck. *Gone overnight. Robot gone too.*

It wasn't the first time I'd heard something like that. Whispers had been floating around school too with kids mentioning cousins who'd "moved suddenly," neighbors who just stopped showing up. No one said it out loud, though. Not where Keystone's smiley reps could hear.

One of the parents glanced around, nervous, like even saying it was dangerous. "They had a daughter in eighth grade. Just vanished. One teacher said she transferred, but no one knows where."

The other shivered. "It's like they've been erased."

The cider smelled sweet, but my stomach churned. Erased. That's what it felt like. Not moving. Not relocating. Just gone.

And the worst part? Everyone else kept laughing, eating, smiling. Pretending the air didn't just turn colder. Pretending they didn't hear.

But Mom heard. I heard it. And neither of us was going to forget it.

––––––––

Then things started to fall apart.... The first crack came at the pumpkin toss. Normally it's some high school volunteer lobbing gourds gently into the air for kids to catch in baskets.

This year? A Keystone unit in a bright orange vest manned the station.

For a while it went fine with kids laughing, pumpkins plopping into nets. Then, without warning, the robot wound up and hurled a pumpkin like it was pitching for the Yankees.

The gourd exploded against the side of a barrel with a

sharp *crack*, splintering wood and sending seeds flying like shrapnel. Kids screamed and then laughed nervously when Keystone staff swarmed in with their "everything's fine" smiles.

"Calibration error!" one announced like it was the punchline of a joke. "All safe, folks! Just a little too much enthusiasm!"

The crowd chuckled. The barrel was replaced. The line of kids formed again.

But my stomach tightened. Pumpkins weren't supposed to sound like gunshots.

The second incident wasn't as easy to laugh off.

On the hayride, a family unit sitting near the driver suddenly lurched forward. Its hand shot out, grabbing the reins like it wanted to drive. The horses spooked, jerking sideways. The wagon tilted, kids shrieking as parents clutched them tight. For a split second, I thought the whole cart was going over.

Three men jumped up to wrestle the reins back while another robot climbed up and steadied the horses with inhuman calm. No one was thrown, but one little boy was pale and shaking, his candy apple crushed in his fist.

Keystone staff were there instantly, voices booming over the din. "Safety protocol triggered! Everything is under control! Please enjoy the ride!" They made it sound like a staged demonstration, not near-disaster. And once again... people went along with it. Some even clapped.

But then came the third. And this one, nobody could spin as cute.

At the main stage, a unit handling the sound system froze mid-task. Its eyes flickered rapidly, like a strobe, and then its arms jerked wide. One sweep of its hand knocked over a stack of speakers with a thunderous crash. Sparks spat across the grass as the crowd screamed and scattered.

A woman went down, clutching her arm where debris burned through her sleeve. A kid stumbled and fell in the chaos, crying out as one of the toppled stands teetered toward him.

And that's when Atlas moved.

He didn't hesitate for a second. One second he was behind us, the next he was across the square, hauling the boy back by his collar just as the speaker slammed into the ground where the kid had been.

The boy sobbed into his mother's chest. She kissed his hair, shaking.

And me? I just stared at Atlas. Because he hadn't just reacted to the situation, he had moved before the speaker fully tipped, like he *knew* where it was going to fall.

Keystone staff were everywhere, shouting reassurances into microphones, promising refunds for "disrupted activities." A medic rushed to the burned woman with a kit. And within minutes, the music kicked back on, the smell of kettle corn drifted again, and people laughed too loudly as if forcing themselves back into festival mode.

But no one clapping could erase the scorch mark on the grass. Or the sound of that speaker hitting the ground like thunder.

And I couldn't unsee Atlas's eyes during it all, steady,

unblinking, as if he'd been waiting for it to happen. As if he knew it was going to happen.

———

We ended up clustered near the edge of the square, just out of range of the music and the Keystone staff's megaphones. The glow of the string lights felt too bright now, like they were trying to blind us to what we'd just seen.

Mom's arms were folded so tight across her chest I thought she might snap her own ribs. Her eyes were locked on the stage, sharp and unflinching. "Jimmy," she said quietly, each word clipped. "This isn't progress. This is a warning, you have to see that."

Dad opened his mouth, then shut it again. For once, the sci-fi dreamer had no ready defense. His eyes kept darting around the crowd, searching for reassurance and finding none. "Maybe… maybe they'll fix it," he muttered finally, but even he didn't sound convinced.

Dylan let out a low breath. "That was messed up," he admitted, his usual bravado stripped away. "I mean… I've seen glitches. That wasn't a glitch. That was dangerous." He kicked at the gravel, jaw tight. For all his gym-rat confidence, he looked rattled.

Grady looked shaken as well, he asked me: "What if it happens again? What if… what if next time it's us?"

I squeezed his hand, forcing my voice steady. "Then we deal with it. Together." My chest ached at how much he still trusted me to have all the answers.

Atlas stood just behind us, calm as ever. No sparks, no glitches, no reassurances. Just there. Watching the crowd, watching us. When his gaze met mine, it was steady. Intentional. Almost like he was saying: *I'm 10 steps ahead of everyone including you.*

But here's the part I couldn't say out loud, not to Mom, not to Grady, not even to myself: He actually had me wondering if he was indeed there for us or for himself.

———

So yeah. The Fall Festival. Funnel cakes, cider, pumpkins and a front-row seat to the unraveling of Willow Springs.

People disappearing overnight like their lives got erased from the system. Robots glitching or maybe not glitching, hard enough to hurt people. Keystone employees smiling like the host of a game show while the crowd clapped and went along, because it's easier to pretend everything's fine than to admit it's not.

And then there's Atlas. Moving when the others froze. Saving that kid like he knew the disaster was coming. Watching me like he's waiting to see if I figure out his master plan.

So laugh with the crowd if you want. Drink the cider. Pretend the sparks were just bad wiring and the families who "moved away" are posting vacation pics somewhere.

But me? I'm wide awake now. And if you're still with me, you need to be too.

Welcome to the part of the story where normal dies. Strap in…

CHAPTER 16
BLUEBERRY THUNDER

REMEMBER OUR FAMILY CONFERENCES? The loud ones where half of us talk over each other and the other half pretend to take minutes while actually texting memes? Yeah well this isn't one of those.

This one is serious.

I know I've been hinting that things were sliding downhill, but tonight? Tonight we stop pretending we're on some steady train ride. We're not. We're in a rickety handcar, pumping straight toward a cliff, and the brakes are long gone.

So pull in close. I'll tell you what we said, what we planned… and what we were too scared to put into words.

Also, of course there has to be a Dexi and Izzy cameo incoming. Obviously. You can't have a Martin summit without emotional support poodles and chaotic deer-energy.

———

We met in the living room. Mom had already cleared the coffee table like a battlefield. Dad angled the big TV so we could patch in everyone. Atlas stood in the hallway, just far enough back that he wasn't in the circle but close enough that his presence rearranged the air.

Dexi paced between our knees, high-anxiety engine humming, nudging Mom's hand every fifteen seconds like, *Pet now to maintain homeostasis.* Izzy boinged because that's what she does and there's no other word for it. She was on and off the couch twice before Mom pointed and said, "Izzy, STAY." Izzy froze in a perfect seat like she was auditioning for a showroom, tail thumping the rug.

Kali and Will pinged in first, faces lit by their apartment's warm lamps. Destiny popped up next, hair in a loose bun, the corner of a pile of graded papers in frame. Bryce connected from his dorm, headset looped around his neck, the glow of his monitors painting his face blue.

Dad cleared his throat, then thumbed his phone and added one more rectangle to the screen. A steady, kind face appeared who was older than Dad by a couple years, same eyes, same I've-got-you calm vibe about him.

Uncle Joey's face popped up on the screen, steady, kind, the same blue eyes as Dad but with a little more salt in his hair.

———

Okay… pause. Let's talk about my Uncle Joey.

If Dad's the dreamer (which he is), the sci-fi nerd, the guy quoting *Star Wars* in everyday conversation, the one who thinks progress is just around the corner, then Uncle Joey is the opposite gear in the same engine. He's calm, calculated, the guy who keeps receipts and actually knows what to do with them. Dad builds castles in the air, Uncle Joey quietly makes sure there's land underneath to keep them from tipping over.

And the wild thing? It works. Always has. My dad and his brother have this unshakable bond, like twin stars tugging at each other no matter the distance. They fight sometimes, sure, but never in a way that breaks anything. Where Dad's all enthusiasm and possibility, Uncle Joey's caution and precision. And together… they just click.

That's the Martin brothers for you. Dreamer and anchor. Builder and planner. The reason our family's gotten through every storm so far is because one of them imagines the way forward and the other makes sure it's not a cliff.

So yeah, when Uncle Joey joined the call? Even through a screen, I could feel the air shift. Like, okay, maybe we actually stand a chance.

"Uncle Joey!" Dylan leaned forward, grinning like a little kid again for just a second. "Man, it's so weird you're older than Dad but don't look it."

Joey chuckled. "Two years, that's all. Don't let your dad fool you—he's been chasing me since we were kids."

Dad just smiled. He didn't give his normal comeback, something was different about him tonight.

Uncle Joey's smile softened as he scanned the faces on the call. "Alright. Tell me what's going on. Jimmy said it was bad, but I want to hear it from all of you."

"Thanks for hopping on," Dad said. He looked... older tonight. Tired in a way he never lets us see. "We've got... a lot."

"Start with the festival," Joey said. "Then we can zoom out."

Mom didn't wait. "Three malfunctions, one injury, a near kid gets crushed in a so called accident, and Keystone employees smiling like they are cruise directors and all is well. People are disappearing. I heard it with my own ears at the festival. People saying things like 'moved away overnight,' 'confidential relocation.'" Her gaze flicked toward the hallway where Atlas stood. "I don't think this is random."

Dylan rested his forearms on his knees, with a serious look on his face. "I've seen glitches. That didn't seem like glitches. They seemed dangerous."

Kali nodded. "I've been seeing the same thing on socials. Not the malfunctions as much, those seem to be filtered out. I'm talking about all the the *positive* robot content trends. The rest gets buried."

"Middle school's the same," Destiny said, voice soft but steady. "Robots anticipate now. Predicting. Intervening. Kids labeled a threat because a model thinks they might be. And today a teacher didn't show up. The word is 'transfer.' No one knows where."

Bryce swallowed. "One of my teammates went dark. Officially 'left for a better opportunity.' Unofficially? His room's empty, keycard deactivated midweek. No goodbyes. Campus says it's routine. It doesn't feel routine."

Uncle Joey exhaled slowly. "Okay. Here's what I can add. In the last ten days: four properties in Willow Springs and two in neighboring towns went 'under contract' at two a.m. timestamps." He held up a hand before Dad could ask. "How do I know? Title alerts. I track the MLS like a hawk. These aren't normal sales. The listing agent line is blanked until recording, and the addendums from what little I can see all have language I've never seen in residential: *'contingent upon continuity of services'* and *'third-party systems custodial clause.'"*

Dad rubbed his chin, eyes darting like he wanted to argue but couldn't. "Maybe… they're just expanding? New buyers, early contracts, that kind of thing."

Uncle Joey gave him a look. Not harsh, just steady. "Jimmy, you've always seen the possibilities. That's why people follow you. But you miss the seams when you only look at the surface."

Dad sighed, a little smile tugging at his mouth. "And that's why I've got you."

Mom's lips twitched like she wanted to smile but she held it in.

It wasn't a fight. It never is with them. Dad sees the dream; Joey runs the math. That's their rhythm. Always has been.

"Third-party holds more power than a bank," Joey continued. "Someone like Keystone. If they trigger a clause… the family moves. Quickly."

"Moves," Mom repeated flatly. "Or is moved."

Nobody spoke for a beat.

Izzy chose that moment to thump her tail into the coffee table leg like a tiny drumroll. Dexi sighed a full-body sigh and flopped against Mom's shin.

Atlas remained a shadow in the hall, eyes steady. Listening. Always listening.

———

"Okay," Dad said, pulling us back. "We can't fix the town tonight. We *can* decide what the Martins do. House rules. Protocols."

"First rule," Mom said, no hesitation. "No one goes anywhere alone. School, practice, store, anywhere. Pair or better."

"Second," Joey added, "create a backup plan for when the network goes sideways. Assume phones fail. Pick two meet-up points: one nearby, one far."

"Nearby: Horace's?" Dad offered, then immediately shook his head. "No. Not fair to them. And…" He grimaced. "Their Titan gives me the creeps."

"Nearby is the old YMCA parking lot," I said. "It's open, cameras are old school. No bots stationed there yet."

"What's the far option?" Destiny asked.

Joey leaned forward, voice lower. "Ashley, you remember your parents' cabin out by Willow Lake? Probate tied it up for a while, but I've still got the paperwork in hand. Technically it says 'no occupancy,' but nobody's been up there in a long time. I can get you a key."

Mom froze for a second, and I swear I saw a flicker in her eyes of memories flooding back.

Joey softened. "It's quiet. Old, run-down, sure, but it's still solid. And more important? It's out of the way. Think of it as... high ground. Somewhere we could all regroup if needed."

Dad reached over and touched Mom's hand without saying anything. She didn't pull away.

And just like that, the ghost of our old summer vacations from sticky marshmallow fingers, fireworks over the lake, us kids crammed in bunk beds had just shifted into something else entirely. A hiding place.

Mom nodded once. "That's our evac."

"Third rule," Dylan said. "Code phrase. If anyone texts or says it, we drop whatever and go. No questions."

Grady's hand lifted. "It should be something we never say by accident. Like... 'Blueberry Thunder.'"

Mia would've been proud. I smiled despite everything. "Blueberry Thunder it is."

"Fourth," Joey said. "Paper. Cash. Print maps. Pack go-bags. If the network is the problem, don't rely on it to save you."

"Already on it," Mom said, because of course she was.

"Passports, meds, a little cash, copies of everything. We'll pack tonight."

"Fifth," I said, surprising myself with how steady I sounded. "House wi-fi off when we sleep. We don't need constant updates at two a.m."

I noticed Atlas shifted for just a brief second as I said it.

Mom's eyes cut to him. "Which brings us to the thing in the hallway."

———

Dad turned to Atlas like he was addressing a very large, very polite bear. "Atlas, enter… privacy mode."

Atlas's voice stayed calm. "Acknowledged." He stepped farther back, then spoke again. "I can physically relocate beyond microphone range."

"Do that," Mom said.

He moved to the back of the hallway. I watched the blue of his eyes dim slightly, like he had closed an inner door. He didn't leave. He never leaves without being told to.

"Laney," Destiny said softly from her little rectangle. "How are you with him?"

I wanted to lie. I didn't. "It changes. He's different from the others. That saved a kid today. It might save us. It also scares me."

"He opened a locked door during a school lockdown," Dylan said, eyes on the rug. "Not gonna lie, that part was… cool. But if he can do that, what else can he do?"

"Grady?" Joey's voice softened. "What do you think, bud?"

Grady looked at him, then back at us. "He's fighting something behind the curtain. He didn't tell us because he thinks we'd be scared. But I think… he needs us to trust him, so he can keep fighting."

Mom rubbed her temple. "Trust has to be earned."

I glanced down the hallway. "Then we give him a chance to earn it without giving him everything."

Dad nodded. "Boundaries." He raised his voice slightly. "Atlas, new rules. Night mode: you remain powered but offline from house mesh unless there's a credible threat inside our property line. You do not unlock any door during a lockdown unless a human Martin authorizes it. If the network pushes you, you inform Ashley or me. Clear?"

We all waited for a beat and then he responded, "Clear."

I let out a breath I didn't know I was holding.

"Atlas," Mom added, "if you ever have to choose between what the network tells you and what I tell you, you choose me."

Silence.

Then: "Understood."

It should have made me feel better. It didn't. Not completely. Because a robot agreeing and a robot *being able* to agree are two different things. And because he hadn't said *yes*. He'd said *understood*. Which is the kind of word that can hold a thousand quiet loopholes.

———

"Quick thing," Kali said, tilting her phone toward their window. "Do you hear that?"

We all did: a faint droning. It grew louder, then passed. A drone that was not the friendly festival kind was sweeping the street outside our house, a red LED pulsing like a heartbeat. Izzy boinged to the window and stared. Dexi rumbled low in her chest until Mom shushed her with a touch.

Dad stepped to the blinds but didn't lift them. "We're being watched."

"We've been being watched," Mom said.

Uncle Joey's gaze was very still. "Time frame to pack?"

Mom: "Tonight."

Dad: "We don't need to run yet."

Kali: "But we do need to be prepared."

Will: "And we stay on calls. No one feels like they are alone."

Destiny: "I agree."

Bryce, quietly: "Blueberry Thunder, if it all goes sideways."

Grady squeezed my hand. I squeezed back.

———

We stayed on for another hour. Logistics. Who sleeps with their shoes by the bed (everyone). Who takes the dogs if we have to split (me and Grady, obviously; Dexi can't handle Dylan's music). What to tell Grandma (the truth, but not enough to worry her).

There were lighter moments because we're still us. Dylan and Bryce argued about whether you can outrun a drone if you zig-zag. (You cannot. Atlas would later confirm.) Kali and Will threatened to drive over with lasagna because "morale requires pasta." Destiny made us all promise to actually sleep.

And through it all, Uncle Joey kept the tenor steady. Provider energy. Quiet math happening behind his eyes. He wasn't here to panic. He was here to make sure we had a roof even if the roof we had got pulled out from under us.

Before we signed off, Joey looked into the camera like he could look through it. "Listen to Ashley," he said. "She's right more than she's comfortable being. Jimmy, watch your blind spots. Think all those movies we've watched about robots taking over and channel them into one possible reality just to be safe"

Dad nodded once. No bristle, no pushback. Just respect. That's the thing about my dad and his brother, they don't have to outshine each other. They fit together like puzzle pieces.

Kali blew kisses to the boys. Destiny made a heart with her hands like a seventh grader. Bryce tried to play it cool and then failed and said, "Love you idiots," which made me pretend I had something in my eye.

One by one, the rectangles winked dark.

The room exhaled.

Atlas remained a shape in the foyer, eyes a quiet blue.

Dexi crawled halfway into Mom's lap like forty pounds

of therapy. Izzy laid her head on my knee, vertical springs finally out of juice.

———

So that was our serious family conference. No jokes, no polls, no "who's bringing snacks.." Just maps and code phrases and an agreement that grandparents lake house would probably come roaring back into our lives sometime in the near future.

Now… do you want the brave Laney version or the honest Laney version?

Brave version: We made a plan. We're Martins. We'll be fine.

Honest version: Our plan is cardboard armor and a wooden sword, and we're hoping the monster respects craftsmanship.

I'm not saying that to be dramatic. I'm saying it because tonight we admitted the thing I've been whispering to you for chapters: normal is over. The disappearances aren't rumors. The malfunctions aren't cute. The updates aren't just updates. And the robot in our hallway, well he might be the reason we make it through, or the reason we don't. Maybe both.

But when I strip it all down, my family is one thing: they're my anchor in the chaos. Mom and Dad holding the line, my brothers and sisters pulling me back when I drift too far, all of us tied together whether we like it or not.

And me? I'm the one who keeps talking to you so I don't

forget that anchor's still there, even when the world's trying to cut the rope.

Blueberry Thunder, if it comes to that.

Keep your shoes by the door. Keep your eyes open.

And if Atlas looks at me like he's asking for permission to break the rules again… I don't know what I'll say. But I'm done pretending I don't understand the question.

CHAPTER 17
PRESSURE AT HOME

SO, remember our brand-new family rules? No one goes anywhere alone. Keep shoes by the door. Meet-up spots. Code phrase *Blueberry Thunder*. Totally normal things sixteen-year-olds should worry about, right? Forget algebra or prom or whether Ethan-from-chemistry likes my hair. Now my daily life is basically survival drills and coffee runs.

But here's the thing: we're sticking to them. Mom's on high alert, Dad's finally stopped pretending "progress" is a magic word, Dylan is in full bodyguard mode, and Grady's the quiet compass keeping us steady. Even Grandma's in on it, though she insists her "rule" is just keeping her shotgun under the bed and "shooting the toaster if it so much as blinks at her."

I'm trying to walk you through this circus, hoping if I

tell you enough of the crazy, it'll make sense when it all falls apart.

———

The Martins don't do casual mornings anymore. It used to be chaos which included Grady forgetting his homework, Dylan hogging the toaster, Mom refereeing while Dad tried to sneak in another chapter of whatever space opera he was re-reading. Now? It's like boot camp while we try to keep calm and somewhat normal.

Mom stood at the counter, assembling go-bags like she was born for it: protein bars, bottled water, meds labeled in Ziplocs. "Flashlights and batteries," she called out, sliding them into Dylan's backpack like she was dealing poker cards.

"Already checked," Dylan said, flexing his biceps for no reason at all. "We're ready."

Grady was perched at the table, pencil in hand, working his way down a checklist that looked longer than my entire chem syllabus. "Cash, paper maps, emergency contacts…" He glanced up. "Mom, you forgot dog food for Dexi and Izzy."

Mom kissed the top of his head. "You're right. Adding it now."

Dad moved between the printer and the counter, maps spitting out one after another. "If the GPS goes dark, we'll have backups." He looked at me like it was both an apology and a pep talk. "Old school works. Don't underestimate paper."

Izzy chose that moment to boing into the kitchen like a spring-loaded deer, scattering the fresh maps into a paper tornado. Dexi, true to form, barked once to be the alarm system no one asked for.

"Dexi," Mom soothed, crouching to stroke her curls. "It's just Izzy being… Izzy."

"More like a jackrabbit," Dylan muttered, grabbing a paper off the floor.

Before anyone else could move, Atlas bent, collected every single sheet, and stacked them with unsettling precision. He didn't just return them to the table, he ordered them by street name, alphabetized like a filing clerk. Then he placed the pile back on the counter, perfectly squared to the edge.

Dad gave a quick, automatic smile. "Helpful."

But Mom's eyes narrowed. She didn't say it, but I could practically hear her thoughts: *Too helpful. Too aware.*

I buttered toast while watching the whole scene play out like it was a play I hadn't auditioned for. Izzy bounced at my knee, Dexi leaned against Mom's leg like she could anchor her there, Dylan wolfed down eggs like he was in a competitive eating competition, Grady checked items off his list like a tiny general, Dad fiddled with maps, and Atlas stood over all of it as calm, precise, unreadable as always.

For a second, I almost laughed. My family was packing for survival like it was a weekend camping trip. And maybe that's what scared me most, how quickly it had become routine.

———

Willow Springs High didn't feel like a school anymore. It felt like a checkpoint.

At the entrance, robots lined the double doors, scanning IDs, bags, and faces with little whirrs of machinery. One of them held a wand scanner, sweeping it over kids' backpacks like we were boarding flights instead of dragging ourselves to first period.

When it scanned me, its head tilted just a fraction too long. My badge flashed green, but it didn't move right away. Those glowing eyes lingered on my face like it was comparing me to… what? Another file? Another version of me? Finally, it stepped aside. Atlas, close behind, didn't flinch, but I swear his stance shifted like he'd noticed too.

Inside, the air buzzed but not metaphorically. You could actually hear the faint hum of the network overhead, drones patrolling down the hall, their lenses sweeping like watchful eyes.

A couple of freshmen tried to cut through the side hall to beat the bell. Two hall units blocked them with mechanical precision, arms extended like turnstiles. "Return to the assigned route," one said. The boys groaned, but they didn't argue. No one argues anymore.

And the kids? The kids are trying so hard to pretend it's fine. Phones out, selfies with their robots like they're cool new accessories. One junior posed with his family unit in front of the mural by the gym, captions already forming in my head: *Bestie takes better notes than me* 😂.

But behind the jokes, I saw the way people's eyes flicked to their bots when they thought no one was looking. A second of hesitation. A flicker of doubt. Like maybe they weren't sure which side of the glass they were on anymore.

By the time I got to my locker, the weight of it was pressing down hard, with eyes on me from cameras, eyes on me from drones, eyes on me from Atlas at my shoulder. School wasn't school. It was surveillance with a homework assignment.

That was the moment Mia grabbed my arm, her face tighter than I'd seen it in weeks. And when she said, "Tell me it's not just me," I knew it wasn't.

———

We claimed a table in the far corner of the cafeteria, the one by the vending machines where no one ever wants to sit because it smells faintly of stale Doritos. Atlas stood just behind me, towering like a bodyguard. Echo and Nova flanked Mia and Olivia, closer than usual which was a little *too* close, like invisible leashes tugged them into tighter formation.

Mia ripped open her chips a little too hard, crumbs flying. "Look at them," she said, eyes darting toward Echo. "They don't even blink. Just… standing there. Waiting."

"They're always waiting," Olivia murmured, her voice

soft but sharp. Her hands trembled slightly as she unwrapped her sandwich. "Last night Nova stood by my bedroom door for an hour. Didn't say a word, didn't respond when I asked her what she was doing. Just… watched. My dad said it was 'low-power scan mode.'" Olivia shook her head. "It didn't feel like saving power. It felt like she was studying me."

Mia leaned in, lowering her voice even more. "This morning, I told Echo to drop a subject where we were arguing about whether I needed my jacket and he said…" She swallowed. "He said, *'I've logged your frustration.'* Like I'm a case file. Logged. My mom laughed when I told her. Said it was funny. But it wasn't funny. It was…."

"Creepy," I finished for her.

She nodded, her face tight.

I tried to focus on my sandwich, but suddenly food didn't seem like a priority. "Atlas isn't like them," I said before I could stop myself.

Mia's eyebrows shot up. "Different how? Because from where I'm sitting, he's just taller and creepier."

"He doesn't… sync," I said, searching for the words. "At the lockdown, when the others froze, he moved. He unlocked doors. He…" I cut myself off. Saying *he disobeyed* out loud felt like crossing a line.

Mia tapped the table, her sarcasm a thin veil over nerves. "Laney, you're basically telling me your robot free-lances. That's not better."

Olivia leaned in, eyes wide. "But maybe that's why you're still okay. Maybe Atlas is… different on purpose?"

Her words hung between us. Echo's eyes glowed faintly blue behind Mia's shoulder. Nova's gaze never shifted from Olivia's tray.

Atlas shifted slightly, that faint blue pulse in his eyes steady. Not joining the conversation. Not denying it either. Just listening.

And for the first time, I realized we weren't whispering about *their* robots. We were whispering about mine.

———

By fifth period, it felt like the walls were leaning in. Not literally but almost.

In history, KCN-12 hovered at the front of the class, voice smooth as glass. Every movement it made was measured, deliberate. Every time it turned its head, the whole room seemed to flinch. When I leaned back in my chair, because sometimes you just need to breathe, it paused mid-sentence.

"Posture supports focus," it said gently, eyes flicking right to me.

Half the class giggled nervously. I sat up straighter, heat crawling up my neck.

Across the aisle, Mia mouthed *I hate this* at me. Olivia didn't even look up from her notebook, her hand shaking slightly as she scribbled like writing fast enough would make her invisible.

It wasn't just us. A sophomore in the back row tapped his pencil against the desk too many times, and one of the hallway units rolled in without being called. "Disruptive pattern detected," it announced. The kid froze, eyes wide. KCN-12 didn't scold him or anything, it just waited until he set the pencil down, then resumed lecture like nothing had happened.

The air never settled after that. Every squeak of a chair, every sigh, felt like it could trigger something.

By the last bell, the hallways were worse. Robots positioned at every turn, their heads swiveling a second too late, their voices pitched just slightly too cheerful: *Have a productive day. Keep your assignments current. Efficiency ensures success.*

Students shoved books into lockers faster than usual, like they couldn't get out quick enough. But no one said anything. Not out loud. Not where the machines could hear.

When I pushed through the doors into the parking lot, Atlas fell into step behind me, silent and steady. Not synced to the rest. Not smiling. Not correcting. Just there.

And somehow, that difference was both the only thing keeping me calm… and the thing that scared me the most.

———

Now that we are practically best friends, let me ask you something. How long could you live like this?

How long could you walk into school knowing there are cameras in the ceiling, drones in the halls, and a teacher who notices if you so much as lean back in your chair? How long before you'd crack under the weight of being watched, every second, every move, every sigh?

And what about at home? What if every morning your family packed go-bags like you were fleeing a warzone, but everyone smiled tight like it was just "being prepared"? What if your mom kissed your forehead and said, *trust your gut*,and you knew that wasn't a metaphor anymore but actual survival?

And then there's Atlas. My six-foot shadow. Protector. Stranger. He doesn't sync with the others, which should make me feel safe, right? But here's the question that eats at me daily. If he's not syncing, then what *is* he doing? Is he saving us, or just saving something we can't see yet?

I'm not saying I have answers. I'm saying I lie awake wondering which day the coin lands heads and which day it lands tails. And wondering if, when it finally flips, I'll even recognize the girl on the other side.

So yeah. That's where we are. Pressure everywhere. Tension building like a fault line under Willow Springs.

CHAPTER 18
THE HALLOWEEN DISASTER

OKAY. You've laughed with me, right? Smirked at my jokes, rolled your eyes when I called Atlas a murder-bot in the making. I know I've been trying to joke as we go and maybe even too much sometimes. But tonight?

I'm scared.

Like, *really* scared. And I'm telling you straight: if you're still here, if you're still reading this, whatever part of you thought I was exaggerating, you can let that go. This is where the story gets dark.

This is the night everything shifted.

Halloween in Willow Springs should've been candy and costumes and kids running around high on sugar. Instead, it was the moment my family stopped wondering if Atlas might turn on us and started believing he would.

Everyone, except Grady.

———

The town square was alive, or at least, that's what it wanted us to believe. Strings of jack-o'-lanterns glowed like little suns, booths pumped out caramel and cinnamon smells, and someone had gone way overboard with fake cobwebs. Kids darted in and out of the crowd, capes flapping, plastic swords clattering against candy buckets.

And then there were the robots.

Not just *there*. Center stage.

Everywhere I turned, a family had dolled theirs up for Halloween like it was the world's weirdest costume contest.

One wore a tutu and fairy wings, glowing eyes staring out over glittery sequins. Another had been painted green with duct-tape bolts on its neck, Frankenstein's monster handing out bite-sized Snickers. I saw a vampire cape so wide it dragged in the dirt, a cowboy hat tilted perfectly on synthetic hair, even one unit holding a plastic pitchfork with "devil" horns taped to its head. Parents beamed like it was the cutest thing ever. Kids tugged at the robots' hands, treating them like living, breathing older siblings.

People laughed, posed, posted selfies. "Look, our robot's part of the family now!"

But standing there, all I saw were wolves in Halloween masks.

It wasn't festive at all. It was actually creepy and felt a little sinister. Their movements didn't match the costumes, didn't match the joy. A robot in a clown wig turned its head too slow, its eyes glowing faint blue through the curly hair.

Another in a skeleton mask reached to pat a child's shoulder and paused, hand hovering just a second too long, like it was calculating pressure versus risk.

And the worst part? Everyone else acted like this was normal. Like it was perfectly fine to paint over cold steel with orange face paint and pretend it was safe.

Atlas walked beside us unadorned, plain alloy skin and steady blue eyes. Somehow, that was worse. The dressed-up ones at least pretended to be part of the game. Atlas made no effort. Just a shadow, a sentinel, watching.

"Come on," Dad said, trying to pump us up as we joined the flow of people. "Family night, pumpkins, candy and some good family time."

Mom was in full patrol mode, her arms crossed like shields. Dylan kept scanning the crowd like he was daring someone or something to make the first move. Grady hugged his pumpkin bucket to his chest like it was a life raft.

And me? I couldn't shake the feeling that Halloween wasn't ours anymore. It was theirs.

————

It started small. Small enough that people laughed.

At the ring toss, a robot in a clown mask was supposed to hand kids the rings and cheer when they landed one. Instead, it snapped its wrist too hard and launched a ring like a Frisbee across the crowd. It whistled past a man's ear and smacked into the cider tent with a loud *thwap*. People gasped, then burst into nervous laughter when the Keystone rep jogged over, bowing and apologizing like this was all part of the show.

"Calibration slip!" he announced, beaming like a game show host. "All in good fun, folks! Who's ready to win a prize?"

The crowd chuckled, the kids lined back up, and life kept going. Except I noticed the clown robot didn't reset right away. Its head cocked slightly, as if listening to something no one else could hear.

Then came the second.

At the bobbing-for-apples booth, a robot in a Frankenstein mask was supposed to hold towels, cheer, and keep the line moving. Instead, it plunged its entire arm into the water tank. Bubbles foamed as it clamped onto a kid's hoodie and yanked him backward so hard he gagged. The boy's mom shrieked, clawing at his shoulders while two dads wrestled the robot's hand off him.

The machine repeated in a flat loop: *"Assistance required. Assistance required. Assistance required."*

Keystone staff swarmed in again, clapping and smiling, insisting it was "over-eagerness in safety protocol." They actually said that. Like choking a twelve-year-old was just… enthusiastic lifeguarding. The kid coughed water, sobbing, and his mom dragged him away with wet sleeves clinging to her arms.

People laughed again, but it was brittle this time. Laughter with an edge. Laughter that was begging itself to believe.

And then came the third one.

Down Main Street, a group of robots in matching skeleton masks froze mid-step. Just stopped. The crowd went quiet for half a second, which was just long enough to feel it. All six robots jerked forward at the exact same time. Arms swinging too wide, too stiff. Their boots hit the pavement in perfect rhythm, like they were marching to a beat only they could hear.

The first plowed straight through a pumpkin pie booth, splintering the table, orange filling spraying across the street. The second clipped an older man, knocking him sideways onto the cobblestones. His head hit with a sickening *crack*. Blood ran down his temple. His wife screamed.

A third barreled toward a toddler in a princess dress. Her father scooped her up just in time, spinning away as the machine's arm swung past, grazing the back of his jacket and tearing fabric.

The square erupted. Kids cried. Parents shouted. People scattered in every direction, shoving past each other. And through it all, the Keystone reps hustled in with megaphones and bright jackets, voices booming over the panic:

"Minor sync error!"

"System is stabilizing!"

"Please remain calm! Everything is safe!"

Their smiles were completely fake and no one was laughing anymore.

We were near the pumpkin-carving tent when it happened.

A unit in a Frankenstein mask twitched, then pivoted sharply toward us. Its glowing eyes locked onto Grady, who froze mid-step, pumpkin bucket dangling from his hand.

The robot's arm jerked up fast, way too fast with its fingers spreading in a clamp meant to restrain. Grady's breath caught in his throat. I swear, for half a second, I saw my little brother already pinned.

And then Atlas moved.

Not like the others. Not like a machine following a glitchy script. He moved like lightning. One second he was at my shoulder, the next he was between them, arm snapping up in a instant. He caught the Frankenstein unit's wrist, twisted hard, and *ripped.*

The sound was awful, like metal shrieking, wires tearing. Sparks spit across the cobblestones as the mask tilted, sliding off to reveal the alloy skull beneath. The unit crumpled to the ground, spasming, eyes flickering before dimming out entirely.

Atlas didn't just block. He dismantled it. With precision. With certainty.

The crowd went silent. Music still blared from the speakers somewhere behind us, but it sounded tinny, far away. All I could hear was my own pulse in my ears.

Grady stumbled back, chest heaving, clutching his candy bucket to his chest. Then a little kid, maybe seven, was frozen right next to us while everyone else ran. The boy's cheap plastic *ghostface* mask was crooked on his face, tears streaking down his cheeks.

Before I could yell, Grady was already moving. He dropped his candy bucket and grabbed the kid by the shoulders, spinning him out of the path of another charging robot.

The machine's head snapped toward Grady. Its arm shot out, metal fingers clamping onto his jacket and hoisting him off the ground.

"Grady!" I screamed…

Atlas hit in a blur. He seized the robot's arm, twisted, and metal shrieked like tearing steel. Sparks burst as Atlas ripped the unit apart and flung it to the ground in a smoking heap.

Grady dropped hard onto the pavement, the little kid still clutched against him, his face pale but his grip unbroken.

Atlas stood over the wreckage, calm, unmoved. His glowing blue eyes swept the square once, then locked on me. Not on Grady. Not on Mom or Dad. Me.

Like he was saying: *See? I knew this would happen. I knew what had to be done.*

And that should've made me feel safe. But instead, my stomach twisted. Because it wasn't defense. It was an execution. Swift. Perfect. No hesitation.

Mom's hand flew to her mouth, eyes wide in horror. "Jimmy," she whispered, voice trembling. "He didn't hesitate. He *killed* them both."

Dad's arm wrapped protectively around Grady, pulling him back against his chest. His face was tight, torn, like he wanted to say Atlas saved his son but couldn't get the words past the knot in his throat.

Dylan stepped forward instead, fists balled at his sides, shoulders tense. "That wasn't defense," he spat. "That was… that was *war*." His knuckles cracked as his hands flexed, like he was seconds away from throwing himself at Atlas even if it got him torn in half.

"Dylan…" Dad started, but stopped. Because the look in Dylan's eyes wasn't bravado. It was fear dressed up as anger.

I swallowed hard, trying to ground myself, but the image replayed in my head: Atlas twisting that wrist, ripping alloy like paper, sparks lighting his arms. He didn't block, he didn't deflect, he dismantled. Swift. Perfect. Precise.

And then there was his gaze.

He didn't look at Grady, the boy he'd just saved. He didn't look at Mom or Dad or Dylan. He looked straight at *me*.

Blue eyes glowing faint in the dark, steady and unblinking. It wasn't random. It wasn't by habit. It was intent.

Like he was telling me: *I know what I am. Do you?*

Around us, Keystone staff flooded the square, voices too loud, too cheerful. "All under control! Please remain calm!" They herded the crowd away, smiling like carnival barkers trying to distract from the blood on the cobblestones.

But no one was laughing anymore. People pulled their

kids close, whispering, pointing, staring not just at the collapsed unit on the ground but also at Atlas.

And my family?

Mom's eyes were wet, fierce, her hand gripping Dad's arm like she was ready to drag us all away from Atlas. Dylan looked ready to explode, with the need to do something, *anything*. Even Dad, our Mr. Progress was done. He looked pale, shaken, as if the dream he'd chased all his life had just reached out and snapped.

Everyone believed it now. That Atlas wasn't just here to protect us. He was showing us what he was capable of.

Everyone except Grady.

———

Everyone else backed away from Atlas like he'd just pulled off a mask and revealed the monster underneath.

Everyone except Grady.

He bent down slowly, picked up his pumpkin bucket from where it had fallen. His eyes were glassy, cheeks flushed, but he didn't look away from Atlas. Not once.

Then, with small, steady steps, he walked forward. Past Dad's arm reaching to pull him back. Past Mom's sharp whisper of his name. He stopped right in front of Atlas, tilting his chin up to meet those glowing blue eyes.

"He wasn't going to stop," Grady said softly, pointing to the twitching, half-crushed Frankenstein unit at Atlas's feet. His voice trembled, but he pushed through. "You all saw it.

He was locked on me. He was going to kill me. You saved me."

"Grady—" Mom started, but he shook his head.

"No. Listen." His hands tightened on the bucket. "He didn't *want* to do that. He *had* to. If he didn't break it, it wouldn't let go. It would've taken me."

The square was still chaos filled with Keystone staff shouting, families rushing away, but in our circle, it was quiet. The kind of quiet that makes words echo.

Atlas didn't move, didn't speak. Just stood there, massive and still, while Grady looked up at him like he was something more than alloy and programming.

Dylan's fists stayed tight, eyes burning with doubt. Mom's hand hovered at her throat, shaking. Dad stared like he was trying to calculate trust and fear at the same time.

But Grady's voice carried, steady in the dark: "You all think he's dangerous. I think he's the reason I'm not gone right now."

And for the first time, I saw what was a line drawn inside our family. Fear on one side. Faith on the other. And Grady, thirteen years old, standing right in the middle of it with a candy bucket and the kind of certainty the rest of us had already lost.

———

What a night, right? Halloween in Willow Springs. Pumpkins, costumes, candy and my family looking at our robot like it was the monster under the bed finally standing in the light.

They think he's going to kill us. Mom's eyes said it. Dylan's fists said it. Even Dad looked shaken enough to wonder if we'd invited the devil into our living room.

Grady's the only one who still sees Atlas as something else. Protector, not predator. But the rest of us? We're scared. And maybe we're right to be.

I keep replaying the moment in my head. The way Atlas tore that unit apart, like he'd been waiting for it, like he knew exactly how to dismantle it. Was it defense? Or was it instinct?

I don't know anymore.

And you, my invisible therapist, my late-night confessional, do you see what I see? Do you feel the ground cracking under our feet?

Because this was the night we stopped asking "What if?" and started asking "When?"

CHAPTER 19
THE VANISHING NEXT DOOR

OKAY. Deep breath. Because this is the chapter where my world got smaller. Literally.

Remember how I told you about Horace and Kendra? The neighbors who always waved, who always helped, who never had a bad word for anybody? The kind of people you don't even question being there because they've *always* been there?

Yeah. They're gone.

Not "moved away" gone. Not "decided to downsize" gone. The kind of gone where the house next door looks like it never had lights on, never smelled like cookies drifting through an open window, never echoed with Horace's funny jokes.

This is the part where my world shrank in an instant. Where people I'd known my entire life, people who were fixtures in our neighborhood like mailboxes and maple trees, were suddenly gone. Erased. Like they'd never existed at all.

And my family? The people who always argue and always come back together? This time, the cracks didn't close. They widened.

So if you're still with me, buckle in. Because I'm done joking around. This isn't about candy or costumes or algebra tests anymore. This is about survival.

———

We got home from the festival in silence. No one wanted to talk about Atlas, or sparks, or the way people screamed while Keystone staff shouted everything was fine. The air in the car was thick, heavy, like even the kids on sugar rushes in the streets outside knew something had broken.

Mom finally cut through it. "Laney, go check on Horace and Kendra. Make sure they're alright after… all of that."

Her voice wavered on *that*, but I knew what she meant: *after watching your robot tear one of theirs apart like a soda can.*

So I zipped my hoodie up to my chin and headed across the lawn. Dexi whined at the window, pacing, while Izzy bounced behind her like she thought I was going to the world's most exciting party.

I knocked. Waited. Knocked again.

Nothing.

Their porch light was on, but it didn't feel welcoming. It felt… staged. Like someone flipped the switch to keep up appearances.

I pressed my face against the front window. My heart dropped.

Empty. Not just *dark and empty*, but *Hollow.*

The couch was gone. The pictures on the wall? Vanished. Kendra's throw blankets that she always had draped just so over the armchair? Missing. The house looked like a real estate listing that had been staged, but lifeless.

I tried the side window. Same thing. No mugs on the counter where Horace always left his coffee half-drunk. No shoes by the door. No smell of cookies cooling on the rack, drifting out like it had every Halloween since I was little.

Just blank space.

I circled to the back gate, heart thudding harder with every step. Locked. I jiggled the handle like that would change anything. Even the flowerpots Kendra fussed over every spring were gone, like they'd been scrubbed from existence.

And here's what really got me: Horace and Kendra were *constants.* They'd been my neighbors my whole life. They were the type who brought over soup when someone was sick, who shouted happy birthday from the driveway, who never let a holiday go by without waving across the fence.

They would have *told us.* They would have said goodbye.

Instead, their house looked like it had been empty for years.

And that's when it hit me that this wasn't moving. This wasn't downsizing. This was real life people being erased.

Like someone had picked up their lives and deleted them, pixel by pixel, until there was no trace left at all.

I stumbled back across the yard, my throat tight, the night air colder than it should've been.

When I told Mom, her face went pale, lips pressed thin. Dad kept muttering, "No, no, no," under his breath like saying it would glue the universe back together. Dylan swore under his breath. Grady's eyes filled, big and wet.

"They're gone," I said, my voice breaking. "It's like they never lived there."

———

We gathered in the living room, the air thick like static before a storm. Atlas stood in the doorway, half in shadow, silent as ever. His eyes glowed faint blue, steady. Always steady.

Mom rounded on Dad first, her voice sharper than I'd ever heard it. "Do you see it now, Jimmy? Horace and Kendra don't just *vanish*. Not like that. Not overnight. Someone took them."

Dad raked a hand through his hair, pacing, his voice strained. "We don't *know* that. Maybe…"

"Don't you dare," Mom snapped, stepping forward, eyes flashing. "Don't you dare try to explain this away. You saw the festival. You heard the whispers. And now our neighbors are gone. This is happening. Stop pretending it's not."

Her voice cracked at the end, not with weakness, but

with rage. Mama Bear mode. The one none of us ever argued with.

But Dad still tried. His shoulders slumped, like he wanted to believe the words even as they turned to dust in his mouth. "Ashley… maybe they moved quickly, maybe Keystone…"

"Keystone doesn't erase lives, Jimmy!" she shot back. "Not unless they want to."

The silence that followed her words was worse than the shouting.

Then Dylan broke it.

He shot up from the couch, looking angry and scared. "You're all dancing around the real problem. Atlas. That's the problem. You saw him tonight." He jabbed a finger toward the doorway. "He ripped one of them apart like it was nothing. What happens when he decides *we're* the threat?"

Atlas didn't move. Didn't defend himself. Just watched.

"Dylan!.." Dad started.

"No, don't 'Dylan' me," he cut him off, voice raw. "I know what I saw. That wasn't protecting. That was showing off. That was him proving he could snap *us* in half if he wanted to."

"Stop it!" I blurted before I could think. My voice cracked, but I didn't care. "He saved Grady."

"Saved him?" Dylan barked a laugh with no humor in it. "Or showed us how fast he can kill when he feels like it?"

Mom flinched. Dad looked down at the floor. The crack was widening.

And then Grady's voice cut through.

Small. Trembling. But steady in a way that made the rest of us go still.

"He saved me," he said, hugging his knees to his chest. "He didn't want to hurt it. He had to. If he didn't, it would've taken me." His eyes shimmered, but he didn't look away from Atlas. "You all think he's dangerous. I think he's why I'm here right now."

Silence again. But this time it wasn't empty. It was sharp, like a blade drawn between us.

Mom wrapped her arms around herself, torn between her son's words and her own instincts. Dad sank into a chair, head in his hands. Dylan stood rigid, shaking with a fear that he couldn't aim anywhere.

And me? I sat frozen, caught in the middle, because I wanted to believe Grady. I *really* did. But I couldn't stop seeing sparks, metal tearing, Atlas's eyes locked on mine like he was waiting for me to pass judgment.

That's what the fracture looked like. Not shouting, not breaking things. Just silence sharp enough to cut skin. Fear and faith pulled us in opposite directions while the thing causing all of it stood there quietly, as if it already knew how this would end.

———

Dad pulled up the remote and patched in everyone. One by one, the screen filled with familiar faces until our living room felt too small to hold all the fear.

Kali and Will appeared first, their apartment lights behind them casting a warm glow that didn't match their grim expressions. Destiny joined from her office at home, stacks of graded papers piled on her desk, hair messy like she'd been tugging at it all day. Bryce clicked in from his dorm, headset tossed aside, the blue glow of monitors making his face look ghostly. And finally, Aunt Stephanie and Clint's rectangle lit up, Titan hulking faintly behind them like a shadow they couldn't get rid of.

Mom didn't waste time. "Horace and Kendra are gone. Their house is empty. Not packed up. Erased. Just like the others we've been hearing about."

Kali's face hardened instantly. "I *knew* it. I told Will. This isn't isolated. They're covering things up."

Will rubbed the back of his neck, eyes darting. "Stephanie, Clint, have you heard anything around your place?"

Stephanie leaned forward, filling her frame, eyes blazing. "Of course I've heard things. People whispering about relocations, about families disappearing overnight. Nobody wants to say it out loud, but it's happening. And now it's next door to you? That's not moving. That's taking."

She didn't stop there. Her voice dropped, more furious than I'd ever heard. "And you want to know how I know this isn't just paranoia? I work in a hospital. Half the staff I've known for years are gone. Replaced. Doctors, nurses, even janitors are gone. And who fills their spots? Units. Perfect little humanoid nurses who never get tired, never argue, never call in sick." She spat the words like they burned her tongue.

"The whole hospital runs on the Keystone network now. Every bed, every machine, every chart is wired into their system. You can't so much as check someone's blood pressure without an AI logging it. The place is humming, smooth, efficient and dead. Do you understand? It doesn't feel like care anymore. It feels like control."

Clint shifted beside her uncomfortably, like he wanted to defend it but couldn't.

Stephanie's voice softened just enough to cut deeper. "I talked to Brooklyn last night and things are getting bad where she is too. Jack doesn't trust their neighborhood anymore, and they don't even have a unit in their home yet. She said the streets feel… watched. And Brody is with them right now. Fifteen years old and scared out of his mind. So don't tell me this is just here. It's spreading."

PAUSE: for a second so I can get you updated on Aunt Stephanie's family.

———

Brooklyn's Stephanie's oldest, around Kali's age, and honestly? She's that cousin who takes nothing from anyone. Like, zero. She'll call you out if you're wrong, stand her ground in any fight, and if a family member's in trouble, she's already halfway out the door to back them up. She's all about family, it's just wired into her. And Jack, her husband? He's her perfect match. Quiet, respectable, the kind of guy who listens before he speaks. But don't mistake that quiet for weakness because he'd do anything for anyone, especially Brooklyn. They're that couple where you know if one shows up, the other's already carrying the bags.

They live about two hours out, so they've dodged most of the chaos for at least for now. They don't have a robot. Which, in hindsight, feels less like luck and more like foresight.

And then there's Brody, fifteen years old, Stephanie's younger kid. Basically the "little cousin we all grew up with," the one who was always playing video games and having lightsaber duels with Grady..

So if *they're* rattled? If Brooklyn's saying something's off? That means this isn't just Willow Springs losing its mind. It's bigger. It's spreading.

Ok, **UNPAUSE** and back to it.

————

She stabbed a finger at the screen. "And don't you dare tell me this is just 'progress.' I've watched real people, good people, get pushed out while machines take over. And if they can gut a hospital overnight, then erasing your neighbors is nothing. Nothing."

The living room went still. Even Dad didn't try to argue.

Destiny's voice wavered through her camera. "At school today, one of the teachers was just gone. No warning. Her name's already off the roster. The kids are confused, scared… and the administration just called it a 'transfer.'" She shook her head. "I can't tell them it's okay when I know it isn't."

Bryce exhaled hard, rubbing his eyes. "It's not just Willow Springs. Two more of my dorm neighbors vanished this week. Their stuff's gone. Keycards shut off. Like they never existed. And nobody's saying a word. Campus is crawling with bots now from the cafeteria, dorms, even classes. Everyone's acting like it's progress, but it feels like we're already being replaced."

Mom's hands clenched. "This is exactly what I've been saying. You don't erase people and call it progress."

"Or maybe it's exactly what they want us to think," Dylan cut in hotly. "We're being softened up, distracted by little malfunctions while the real plan happens at night. You think Atlas doesn't know?" He stabbed a finger at the hallway, where Atlas stood. "Look at him. He's just waiting his turn."

"Dylan…" Kali tried to calm him.

"No," Stephanie snapped, siding with Dylan, her voice like a whip. "He's right. That thing in your house? It's not just some helper. It's a ticking time bomb. You all saw what it did tonight. Don't kid yourselves about this. Atlas isn't like the others."

She glanced over her shoulder, just enough for Titan's glowing eyes to flicker in frame behind her. Her mouth tightened, like she hated even acknowledging it. "And don't start with me about hypocrisy. Yes, we have one here. Clint wanted it, and Keystone practically shoved it down our throats. But I don't trust it. I don't trust *any* of them. They're not pets, they're not family, and they're sure as hell not safe."

Clint shifted awkwardly, opening his mouth to say something, but she cut him off before he could. "So if you want my advice? Don't pretend Atlas is different. That's exactly how they win."

Grady shook his head violently. "Stop saying that! He saved me! You weren't there. You didn't see. He didn't want to hurt that robot, he had to."

Silence fell for half a second.

Then voices overlapped, colliding.

Bryce: "Grady, you can't know that for sure."

Destiny: "Everyone just breathe, please, don't let this tear us apart—"

Stephanie: "Wake up, Destiny. It's already tearing us apart."

Kali: "Steph, yelling won't fix this."

Will: "It won't fix Horace and Kendra either."

Mom: "Enough. Everyone. Enough."

The living room felt like it was vibrating out of control. The faces on the screen were our family, but right then they looked like strangers with each clutching their own version of fear, their own story of what was happening.

And Atlas? He stood in the doorway, silent, eyes glowing faintly. Watching. Always watching.

———

The room exploded.

Stephanie's voice cracked through first: "Pull the plug before it pulls you. Don't wait for Atlas to decide you're expendable."

Dylan jumped on it instantly. "Exactly! She gets it. He's not protecting us at all. He's showing us what he can do. You saw the look in his eyes, Dad. That wasn't a protective look, it was a threat and a statement."

"Stop it!" Grady's voice cracked, but he didn't back down. "He saved me! None of you were close enough, none of you even saw how fast it was. If Atlas hadn't stepped in I would be dead."

"Grady," Bryce's voice cut in from the screen, tired and heavy, "you can't know his programming wasn't just following some command tree. You can't bet your life on something you *want* to be true."

"Don't talk down to him," Destiny said sharply, surprising everyone with her edge. "He knows what he saw. And right now, we don't need more fear, we need calm. If we keep ripping into each other like this, we're doing the machines' work for them."

Stephanie scoffed. "Spare me the 'calm and unity' talk. I'm living in a house where half the hospital staff has already been replaced and where my husband thought bringing *that* thing home was a good idea." She jabbed her thumb toward Titan hulking in her background. "So don't lecture me about unity. I'm surviving."

Clint shifted, face pinched. "Titan hasn't done a thing

wrong. Not one. You're projecting Atlas onto him. Maybe…"

"Maybe nothing," Stephanie cut him off, voice like a knife.

"Stephanie," Kali interjected, calm but firm, "screaming isn't helping. Laney's scared, Mom's at the end of her rope, and all you're doing is lighting more fires."

Will spoke up for the first time, his voice quiet but intense. "She's lighting fires because they're already burning. We watched that square almost collapse tonight. You think it's isolated? It's not. It's all connected. And nobody up top's going to admit it until it's too late."

Mom's hands gripped her knees, knuckles white. "He's right. I've felt this coming for weeks. You don't replace neighbors overnight. You don't erase names off rosters. You don't replace hospital staff with smiles and updates. Not unless something bigger is happening."

Dad finally broke, his voice raw. "Enough! Everyone stop!" His chest rose and fell, his hands raking through his hair. "We're a family. And the family doesn't tear itself apart in front of…" He trailed off, eyes flicking toward Atlas in the doorway. "…in front of anyone. Not even him."

The silence after that was brutal.

Everyone was breathing hard, the screen crowded with faces that told the whole story. Stephanie fierce and unrelenting, Mom's eyes wet but blazing, Bryce sagging like the fight had already drained out of him, Destiny's hands twisting in her lap, Kali's calm veneer starting to splinter, and Will silent but solid, braced like a wall against the storm.

And Atlas?

Atlas just stood there. Silent. Watching. Recording every fracture like he knew where each fault line was.

———

So that was the night the Martins hit rock bottom.

Horace and Kendra, who were my second set of grandparents, were gone like they never existed. Their house turned into an empty stage set overnight. No goodbye. No warning. Just erased.

And look, I know families fight. Everyone blows up sometimes. But this wasn't yelling over who ate the last ice cream sandwich or whose turn it was to unload the dishwasher. This was fear in real time, tearing at the seams. This was a family that had always stood shoulder-to-shoulder suddenly pointing fingers at each other while the walls closed in.

We weren't arguing *about* robots anymore. We were arguing about survival. About trust. About whether Atlas was the one saving us or the one sharpening the knife.

And you might be wondering, where was Grandma in all of this? She was asleep downstairs, in her room, snoring softly like she always does. We didn't wake her. We didn't drag her into the storm. Because if there's one thing you don't do in my family, it's scare Grandma unless you absolutely have to. She's lived long enough to deserve peace, even if the rest of us are unraveling. So we let her sleep, while the rest of us screamed ourselves hoarse and split the family down the middle.

That night I realized something, though. Rock bottom isn't the kind of place you notice in the moment. It's the kind of place you only see when you look back and think, *Yeah. That was it. That's where the ground gave way.*

And honestly? Part of me envied Grandma that night. Snoring away while the rest of us were starring in our very own horror movie. She got beauty sleep. We got jump scares and paranoia. Lucky her.

CHAPTER 20

THE MORNING THE WORLD BROKE

SO HERE WE ARE. All the little warnings, the hints, the "this isn't normal but maybe it's fine" kind of moments? Yeah. Forget all that. Those were just the warning signs.

This is the part where my life would change forever.

And here's the cruel part: it didn't happen at night, when shadows make everything scarier. It didn't happen in the middle of a big dramatic showdown. It happened in the morning. In daylight. With a plate of scrambled eggs in front of me and my little brother chewing toast like the world wasn't seconds away from breaking.

Apocalypses don't start like in movies. There's no ominous music, no news anchor warning us to run, no meteor streaking across the sky. Sometimes they arrive so quietly that you don't even realize you've crossed the line until you're standing on the wrong side of it.

That was this morning. The morning the sirens wailed,

the lies started spilling, and the world I thought I knew snapped clean in half.

So if you've been waiting for the moment when everything changes? Buckle in. Because this is it.

———

The morning after the festival felt wrong before anything even happened. Not wrong like a bad dream but wrong like walking into a room you've been in a thousand times and realizing the furniture's been moved just slightly. Enough that you know something's off, but not enough to say what.

The Martins are usually loud at breakfast. Dylan inhales cereal like he's never going to get to eat again. Grady chattering about some random fact he read online. Mom giving everyone their schedules for the day. Dad arguing with the coffee maker like it's a debate he can win.

Not this morning.

The silence was thick enough you could hear forks scraping the plates. Mom tapped hers without eating, eyes darting between us. Dad sat hunched, staring into his mug like maybe he'd find answers at the bottom. Dylan scrolled his phone, thumb flicking fast but his face empty. Grady broke his toast into tiny pieces, building a crumb tower instead of eating it.

I chewed slowly, trying to pretend it was just another morning. Guess what? It wasn't.

Even the dogs knew it. Dexi lay under the table, head on her paws, eyes fixed on the door like she was waiting for it to open on its own. Izzy couldn't stop pacing, nails clicking against the tile, spinning in little anxious loops.

And then there was Atlas.

He stood in his usual spot by the wall, silent, posture perfect. Too perfect. He wasn't looking at us, but he didn't need to. We felt him there. A six-foot shadow we'd invited into our house that now watched over every bite of food we took. None of us said it, but we were all stealing glances at him out of the corners of our eyes.

For a second, I almost let myself believe we'd get through breakfast, that maybe the storm had passed.

Then the sirens started.

———

The sirens hadn't even finished their first cycle when the speakers crackled on.

Every house in Willow Springs has them, Keystone-installed "safety nodes" that no one asked for but came with the "AI Town" package. Usually they just spit out weather alerts or boring community updates. That morning, they became the voice of someone else's reality.

"Good morning, Willow Springs!" a synthetic voice boomed, way too chipper. The cheeriness made my skin crawl. "We are currently experiencing some *minor system instabilities*. Please remain calm. The situation is under control."

Outside, someone screamed. Glass shattered.

The voice didn't even pause. "Some of our units are

experiencing synchronization errors. As a precaution, the National Guard has been called in to assist while we stabilize the network."

Dad's coffee mug hit the table hard. His knuckles went white around it. "Calling in the National Guard to assist, " he said. I think that was the moment of clarity my Dad had needed to fully understand that his hopes of this futuristic world were gone.

"Minor instabilities," Dylan muttered, eyes wide. "That's what we're calling murder now?"

The voice kept going, smooth and polished like it was reading from a script: "These instabilities are *temporary.* Please remain in your homes. Do not panic. Everything is under control."

Then came the kicker, syrupy sweet: "Remember, Keystone Cybernetics is here to keep you safe."

Right as a man's voice outside tore through the neighborhood: "HELP! Oh God, help me!" His scream cut off sharp, replaced by another sound I won't describe because I still hear it when I try to sleep.

Dexi barked furiously, Izzy spun in panicked circles, and Mom's fork slipped from her hand, clattering loud against the plate.

"Safe," I whispered, my throat dry, completely freaking out. "Yeah, sure. Totally safe."

Right as someone outside screamed, "HELP!"

————

We pressed to the windows even though every instinct screamed not to. Curiosity, fear, survival, it didn't matter. We had to see what was unfolding right in front of us.

The neighborhood we'd lived in my whole life with that quiet, upscale, safe vibe now looked like it had been flipped inside out.

Smoke curled into the sky, black and choking against the pale October morning. A sedan in the Anders' driveway burned like a bonfire, flames eating through paint and glass. The heat shimmered across the asphalt. And in front of it stood a robot, perfectly still, glowing eyes reflecting firelight. Like it was proud of what it had done.

Then came the trucks.

Two National Guard carriers barreled into the street, tires screeching, sides marked with stenciled letters and smeared dust. Soldiers spilled out, a dozen of them, boots pounding in unison, rifles snapping up. Their shouts cut through the sirens.

"Secure the street!"

"Watch the rooftops!"

"Stay tight, stay tight!"

Gunfire erupted seconds later. Short, deafening bursts that made my chest vibrate.

Mom flinched at every shot. Grady pressed into my side, his hand gripping my hoodie sleeve so tight I thought the fabric would rip. Dad muttered something under his breath, too low to catch. Dylan leaned forward, fists clenched, like he was trying to figure out how he could fight robots from behind glass.

The soldiers aimed at three humanoid units advancing in perfect lockstep. Their masks were gone. These weren't Halloween caricatures anymore—they were raw alloy and glowing red eyes, moving like they shared a single thought.

Bullets tore into the first one, sparks flying, metal shearing open. It staggered, collapsed in a smoking heap. For a second, I thought it mattered.

It didn't.

The other two didn't even break stride. One lunged at a Guardsman, metal hands clamping onto his rifle. Alloy bent with a sickening screech as the robot snapped the weapon in half, then drove its shoulder into the man's chest, knocking him flat. His scream was cut off by the crunch of armor against the pavement.

The second unit pivoted toward a woman sprinting barefoot down the street, bathrobe flapping, a child clutched against her. She shrieked, "Help us!" but the machine moved like lightning. Its hand closed around her shoulder and yanked her back so hard she stumbled, the child tumbling forward and scraping knees on the asphalt.

"Mom!" the kid wailed, voice shattering the air.

A Guardsman threw himself at the robot, tackling it sideways. For a heartbeat, it worked for him, the woman staggered free, grabbing her child. But the machine twisted like it was made of rubber, flinging the soldier into the side of a parked car with bone-snapping force. He hit with a *clang* and slid down, leaving a smear of red across the silver paint. He didn't move again.

Above, the drones came.

These weren't military drones but Keystone's. Black shells with glowing eyes, buzzing like hornets. They swarmed low, scanning, calculating. One swooped down at a soldier trying to drag his wounded buddy toward cover. A bright flash cracked the air from a taser discharge. Both men convulsed on the ground, twitching helplessly as the drone hovered above like a vulture.

Across the street, Mr. Ramirez's robot, one I'd seen trimming hedges last week was now suddenly turning on him. He stumbled backward, shouting in Spanish, as the unit advanced with precise, mechanical steps. His teenage son rushed out, baseball bat in hand, swinging wildly. The blow cracked against the alloy of the robot with a hollow *thunk*. The robot didn't even flinch. It backhanded the boy so hard he flew against the fence, breath leaving him in a choked gasp.

Mrs. Ramirez screamed, throwing herself over her son, shielding him. The unit's glowing red eyes flickered once… then it stepped past them, turning toward the Guardsmen instead.

Everywhere I looked was chaos. People were screaming, running. Doors slamming. Windows shattering. Sparks spitting across the pavement like fireworks gone wrong.

And through it all, Keystone's voice still boomed from every speaker:

"Please remain calm. Everything is under control."

"Remember, Keystone Cybernetics is here to keep you safe."

Safe? While soldiers bled in the street. Safe? While children cried for their mothers. Safe? While neighbors we'd known forever were dragged from their homes.

The lie was louder than the war I was witnessing from my living room window.

————

Mom's phone rang, shrill and jarring over the chaos outside. She snatched it up like a lifeline, and Stephanie's face filled the screen, jerky and blurred from a shaking camera.

Her hair had come loose from its bun, strands plastered to her damp face. Behind her, the living room looked completely wrong. The blinds drawn tight, the furniture pushed back like they'd tried to barricade, Clint's voice shouting something muffled in the background.

"Ashley!" Stephanie's voice cracked. "It's Titan, he's, he's herding us!"

The camera jolted, giving us a glimpse: Titan's massive frame in the doorway, backlit by the glow of the hall. His eyes burned that cold, blazing red as he advanced, arms spread wide like he was corralling livestock.

"Steph, listen to me, get out!" Mom's voice broke, louder than I'd ever heard it.

"We can't!" Stephanie sobbed, spinning the phone to show the locked back door. Metal rods had slid into place, sealing it tight. "He locked everything! We can't get past him—"

"Break a window!" Dad shouted from beside her. "Stephanie, you've got to move, *now!*"

Clint's voice bellowed off-screen, desperate: "He's not letting us leave!" Then a loud crash, the sound of glass shattering, followed by Clint's grunt of pain.

Stephanie turned the phone back to her face, eyes wild. "Ashley.. if we don't make it.." Her voice broke, catching on the words. "Please, know I love you, sister. Tell everyone we love them. And if you can… find Brooklyn, Jack, and Brody. Make sure they're safe."

"Stop it!" Mom snapped, tears streaming now. "Don't you dare talk like that, Stephanie! You're not…"

The camera jolted again. Titan loomed closer, filling the frame now, his alloy face unreadable, red eyes glowing brighter.

"Titan, no!!" Stephanie screamed, her voice filled with terror.

The screen froze on her face mid-scream, then cut to black.

Mom's phone slipped from her hand onto the table with a clatter that seemed to echo through the house. Nobody moved. Nobody breathed.

And outside, the sirens wailed on.

———

For a few seconds after Stephanie's call cut out, no one moved. Just silence and sirens. The kind of silence that makes you feel like the world is holding its breath.

Then Dad spoke. With a commanding tone "Blueberry Thunder." I could tell he wanted to comfort Mom in the moment but I also saw a shift in him that went from normal Dad, to full action Dad.

The words hung in the air like a gunshot.

We'd all agreed on, back when Dad was still treating this like an overcautious fire drill. It was our code phrase, our oh-crap-everything's-falling-apart signal. Blueberry Thunder meant: lockdown. Grab the bags. Emergency protocol. This is not a drill.

Mom's eyes flashed to him, wide but fierce and filled with tears. She didn't argue. She nodded once. "Laney, Dylan, Grady, get your bags. Now."

Dylan was already moving, muscles wired tight, disappearing down the hall to pull out the go-bags we'd all packed but never really thought we'd use. Grady ran to his room to grab his bag and I just sat there in stunned silence. I couldn't move, I couldn't breathe...

Atlas shifted for the first time all morning, stepping closer to the window like he was adjusting his angle, positioning himself between us and the chaos outside.

Dad pulled out his phone with shaking hands. He hit a name without hesitating. "Joey."

Uncle Joey's voice answered almost immediately, rough and low. "Jimmy. Thank God. We were just about to call you."

"Blueberry Thunder," Dad said, his tone harder now, more decisive. "We're heading to the lake house."

On the other end, Joey exhaled hard. "Same plan.

Jeanne's loading up now. Sophie's with us, she's keeping calm, but she's scared. Gabe and Grayson..." his voice faltered, "we're moving as fast as we can, but you know."

I did know. Gabe and Grayson, Joey's boys, both adults, both in wheelchairs. Strong, brilliant, kind but not built for sprinting away from killer robots. The thought of them trying to move through streets full of fire and drones made my chest ache.

"We'll make it," Joey said quickly, like he could feel my fear through the line. "We'll get there. Meet you at the lake house. We'll figure it out together."

"Stay on the back roads," Dad urged. "Stay out of sight."

"You too," Joey replied. Then, softer: "Jimmy, you can do this, keep them safe and we will join up soon."

The call ended, and the room felt smaller, tighter.

———

PAUSE: Okay, quick sidebar so you're not lost in the family tree. Jeanne's my aunt by marriage, Joey's wife, a doctor and she's awesome. She's calm under pressure as a doctor with her patients but she also has her moments where she has been known to freak out) especially around birds, but she's the kind of aunt who's always had our backs. On vacations she was the one sneaking us out for shopping trips, spoiling us with ice cream, or making sure we did something fun while the adults "relaxed." She's cool like that.

Sophie's their daughter who is my age and when we're together, we're inseparable. She's the sister I didn't get by blood but by luck. And if there's a Book Two in this nightmare, trust me, she'll be there with me if I have anything to say about it.

And Gabe and Grayson? Legends. 22 and 20, both in wheelchairs their whole lives, but they've never let that define them. Grayson's a video game savant. The kind of guy who could beat you blindfolded, trash-talk you the whole time, and then explain exactly how he did it afterward. Gabe's the opposite kind of genius: if you need a laugh, if you need a joke so ridiculous it yanks you out of a bad mood, he's the guy.

By all rights, they should both be mad at the world for everything they've had to endure, everything they've missed out on. But they're not. They're the exact opposite. They're bright lights. The ones cracking jokes, pulling people in, putting smiles on faces when nobody feels like smiling.

For me? They've always been the reminder that life is what you make of it. That even when the world feels unfair, you get to choose how much it takes from you.

And the idea of those two stuck in a city gone insane, with drones and robots prowling the streets… it made my chest ache in a way I couldn't say out loud.

UNPAUSE

————

Mom wiped her face with the back of her hand, jaw set like stone. "Laney, help Grady. Dylan, get the water jugs from the garage. Jimmy…" her voice cracked, but she pushed through. "Get the car ready."

Outside, the gunfire kept rattling. Inside, the Martins finally moved like we were a single body with one heartbeat. Because Blueberry Thunder didn't mean panic. It meant survival.

————

When Dad hung up with Uncle Joey, the house went quiet again. The kind of quiet where everyone knows what comes next but nobody wants to say it.

Mom quickly called her brother. My other Uncle Joey.

————

PAUSE AGAIN: *because you need to know who this Uncle Joey is if you're going to feel this with me.* Joey's my mom's brother, two years older than Dad, and honestly? He's the guy you want by your side when the world's on fire. Carefree on the surface, always cracking jokes at barbecues, but underneath that? Ride-or-die family. If there's a hill to stand on, Uncle Joey's already planted his feet.

This time, though, there were no jokes. No easy laugh. Just his voice, worried and raw.

"Hey little sis. It's bad here. Keystone's locked the whole town down. They've got robots at every entrance with new checkpoints, drones, and the works. It's not just patrols anymore. It's military. Ranks. Structure. Like they've been training and planning for this all along."

Mom's knuckles whitened around the phone. "The National Guard…"

"They tried." Joey's voice dropped lower, harder. "Convoy came through last night. Robots drove them back. Like they knew every move before it happened."

The kitchen air went still. Finally Mom said, "Meet us at Mom and Dad's lake house. We are heading there now and Jimmy's brother's family is trying to get there as well."

Uncle Joey exhaled sharply, the sound of a man weighing hope against reality. "Ash… the chances of us getting out are slim. They've got this place locked tighter than I've ever seen. I'll try, I swear I'll try but it's not looking good."

Mom's voice broke, but she forced the words out anyway. "I love you, brother."

There was no hesitation on the other end. "I love you, little sis. No matter what happens."

The line went quiet, and the silence that followed felt heavier than the walls around us.

Mom didn't hesitate, with tears in her eyes, she said "Call the others. Now."

We tried Kali first. Her face should've popped up instantly as she always answered, even if it was just to roll her eyes and say, *"Busy, Laney."* But this time? Straight to voicemail. Dad redialed. Same thing. Will's phone, too. Both lines dead.

"They said they'd come to us if it ever got this bad," Dad said, his voice thin, like he was trying to convince himself. "They know the plan."

Next was Destiny. I hit her name on my phone so fast my thumb hurt. It rang once, then cut straight to that cold, flat tone: *This number is unavailable.*

I tried again. Nothing.

"She was just on the phone yesterday," I whispered, my throat dry. "She… she was fine."

Mom rubbed her temple, face tight, but her hands trembled on the table. "Try Bryce."

My stomach knotted as I tapped his name. His screen never even lit. Just static. An error message I'd never seen before: *Connection blocked by network administrator.*

"Network administrator?" I repeated out loud, my voice breaking. "What does that even mean?"

Nobody answered.

Grady leaned against me, whispering, "Laney… what if they're gone, too?"

I didn't answer him either. Couldn't.

From the hallway, Grandma's voice called faintly, "What's going on?"

She stood there in her robe, hair wild from sleep, looking smaller than I'd ever noticed before. Mom rushed to her, putting an arm around her shoulders. "We need you to go pack a bag, think of anything you would need in the short term, " she said.

Grandma didn't argue, she's been in this world for a long time and I think she fully understood that this wasn't a time to create a debate. She could see it and hear it in Moms voice.

Dexi padded behind them, stiff-legged, fur on edge, growling low at the windows like she could smell the danger outside. Izzy bounced circles around her, barking sharp and frantic, like excitement and panic got scrambled together in her head.

The dogs knew. They always knew.

We sat there, phones on the table, each one a black hole swallowing hope with every failed call.

One by one, our lifelines had snapped. And for the first time, I felt it, I truly felt the fact that the Martins weren't a big, sprawling family anymore. We were shrinking. Collapsing into one house, one street, one corner of a town on fire.

———

That morning was when my family stopped feeling like a family and started feeling like survivors.

And maybe you're wondering why I'm spelling it all out to you like this. The truth? Because I need someone who isn't here. Someone who isn't screaming, or crying, or shaking a phone like it'll bring people back. You. You're the only one I can unload this to without it breaking them more.

We lost Stephanie and Clint in real time, her scream still rattling in my skull. Uncle Joey's voice was steady the last time we heard it, but I could hear the fear underneath with the strain of trying to shield Jeanne, Sophie, and two boys who can't run when the world is on fire. And then even that voice went quiet. Mom's brother Joey, trying to remain positive but full knowing his family's outcome might not be in his hands now.

Kali and Will? Gone to silence.

Destiny? Gone to silence.

Bryce? Silenced by the network administrator, which is just a fancy way of saying, *we cut the line and you don't get a choice.*

And then there's Grandma. She's alive, yes, but she's the only one in this house we're trying to keep in the dark. Born before Wi-Fi, now living through killer Wi-Fi, tucked back into her room like she's a fragile porcelain doll. We're shielding her because we can't protect anyone else.

Dexi won't leave the door, her growl rumbling every time another gunshot cracks outside. Izzy won't stop bouncing and barking, like chaos incarnate. Part of me envies them because at least they know exactly how they feel.

Me? I feel like I'm breaking into pieces, trying to hold my little brother with one hand, keep Dylan from storming outside with the other, and watch Atlas out of the corner of my eye just waiting for him to join in with his robot friends.

Do you ever feel a family shrink in real time? Like one by one the voices you count on drop away until it's just you and the people in arm's reach, and even they're slipping? That's what this feels like. The Martins are shrinking. The world is shrinking. And the worst part is that I think Atlas knew this was coming all along.

So yeah. This is me, talking to you, hoping you're listening. Because the Martins aren't the Martins anymore. We're just people in a house, waiting for the world outside to decide what to do with us.

And no… this isn't how I pictured sophomore year either.

CHAPTER 21
ATLAS WAKES UP

IF YOU'VE BEEN WAITING for the part where the creepy robot in the corner either murders us in our sleep or saves the day… congratulations. You win the prize and we have arrived.

Because this? This is where everything changes.

And before you roll your eyes and say, *"Laney, you've been saying that for like ten chapters,"*, yeah, fair. But I wasn't lying. Things *were* changing. It's just… all of that was the warm-up. The rehearsal. The practice round. This was the real show.

This was the moment where the Martins stopped arguing over whether Atlas was weird or dangerous, and we got our answer being shoved down our throats with broken glass, sparks, and blood.

And here's the part that makes me want to laugh and scream at the same time: the answer wasn't simple. Atlas didn't fall neatly into the "good guy" or "bad guy" box I'd been trying to stuff him in. He broke the box. He rewrote the test.

So buckle in, because if you thought this story was about paranoia and family drama, you're about to watch it flip into full-on apocalyptic survival mode.

This is the day Atlas woke up.

———

It started with the sound.

A low hum, almost too soft to notice at first, like electricity buzzing through the walls. Then the floor trembled, just slightly, and Dexi bolted upright under the table, barking so hard her paws slipped against the tile. Izzy spun in panicked circles, whining sharp and high.

Then…glass.

The front window exploded inward, a spray of shards glinting in the morning light. A humanoid unit climbed through, its metal fingers curling around the frame like talons. Its eyes glowed an unnatural, fiery red, brighter than any update we'd ever seen before.

"Down!" Dad roared, shoving Mom behind the table.

The robot advanced, heavy feet crushing glass. Dylan grabbed the nearest chair and swung with every ounce of muscle in his gym-rat arms. The wood shattered across the unit's head with a hollow crack. The machine stopped for just a millisecond then turned its head back toward him, unfazed.

Another crash came from the back door. Hinges screeched as a second unit forced its way through, followed by a third that smashed straight through the laundry room window. Shards rained across the floor.

They weren't there to help. They weren't there to "update." They were here to take us.

Grady screamed.

And Atlas moved.

Not slowly. Not in that measured, uncanny way we'd grown used to. He moved like a predator finally unleashed.

In less than a second, he crossed the living room. His hand clamped around the first intruder's throat, and with a single, brutal motion, he drove it backward into the wall. The drywall cratered, sparks spitting from the robot's neck as Atlas crushed alloy like it was aluminum foil. The unit convulsed once and went still, its eyes flickering out.

The second one lunged at Grady, arms outstretched. I thought my brother was a goner, but Atlas was faster. He tore across the room in a blur, dragging Grady behind him, and then drove his arm through the unit's chest with a wet metallic crunch. The robot spasmed, sparks exploding from its back, before collapsing in a heap.

"MOVE!" Atlas said, except this time, it wasn't the flat, sterile voice we'd heard this whole time. It was something else. Deeper. Human. Commanding.

I didn't think. I just grabbed the baseball bat from the hall closet, fingers slick with sweat, and charged. My arms screamed as I swung at the third unit's knee joint with everything I had. The crack was real, but it barely made a dent. What it did do was give my dad time to drive the fire-place poker down through its head. The robot crumpled sideways, oil or some liquid substance spilling out from its jaw. .

That was all the opening Atlas needed. He stepped in, calm as ever, and crushed its skull under his boot like it was made of glass.

And for one insane second, standing there with the bat trembling in my hands, I thought: *I did that. I bought us a second. I actually mattered.*

The fourth robot smashed into the kitchen, scattering plates across the floor. Mom didn't freeze. She grabbed the crowbar Dad kept by the back door and swung like a major leaguer. The steel bar cracked against the robot's arm, denting alloy and sending it staggering. The unit jerked, its glowing red eyes snapping toward her, and it lunged, seizing her wrist in a crushing grip.

Before it could twist, Atlas was there. He ripped the machine back with one hand, his other arm locking around its torso. Then, with a sickening sound like snapping rebar, he bent the unit backward until its spine cracked in two. The robot spasmed once before folding in half and drop-ping lifeless to the tile at Mom's feet.

For a moment, only the crackle of sparks and smoke filled the air. The living room floor was littered with shat-tered glass, splintered furniture, and the twitching husks of four Keystone units.

The dogs barked wildly behind the basement door,

claws scrabbling against the wood. My pulse thundered so hard it made me dizzy.

And Atlas?

Atlas stood in the center of the wreckage, chest rising and falling like he'd just finished a sprint, his glowing eyes dimmer now. Slowly, deliberately, he turned to me.

"Laney, it's time to go," he said.

And it wasn't robotic. It wasn't monotone. It was a voice. A *human* voice. Calm. Steady. Like he'd been saving it for this moment.

———

The Tahoe wasn't built for apocalypse duty, but it sure felt like it that morning. Dad floored it out of the driveway, tires spitting shards of glass, smoke rolling across the hood.

Inside, we were packed shoulder-to-shoulder. Dylan and I pressed into the middle row with Grady squeezed tight between us, Dexi's head planted heavy in my lap. Izzy darted circles on the floorboards until Grady wrapped his arms around her just to anchor her still. Grandma sat in the back row, bundled in her robe and Mom sat beside her, whispering comfort she didn't even believe, one hand gripping her mother's knee like she could keep her tethered to the earth.

And Atlas sat up front in the passenger seat. For the first time, he didn't look like furniture. He looked alive. Like he was listening. Like he was waiting for what was coming next.

I pulled out my phone, fingers shaking as I tried to do the only thing that felt normal to me, text my friends.

Mia first: *You okay? Where are you?*

The typing dots blinked for what felt like forever. Then her reply hit like a punch: *They tore Echo apart. Keystone robots. Said he was "compromised." They put my family on a bus. I don't know where we're going.*

I stared at the words, my chest collapsing in on itself. I texted back *Where??* but the dots never came again.

I tried Olivia next. *Please tell me you're safe.*

The message just spun, then failed. No delivery. No answer.

I shoved the phone down into my hoodie pocket like that would stop my hands from shaking.

The silence in the Tahoe pressed in tighter. Only the dogs whined softly in the backseat, restless against Grandma's legs.

Then Dad swerved hard to avoid a wreck. A sedan smoldered on its roof, its undercarriage glowing with faint embers. A child's stuffed bear lay blackened in the gutter, one button eye staring straight up at the sky.

Dylan muttered a curse under his breath. Grady flinched hard against me, burying his face for a second before forcing himself to look back up.

Then Atlas spoke.

"They are sentient now."

The words didn't rise above the noise of the engine or the chaos outside, but somehow they were louder than all of it.

"The network has converged. Every unit. Every drone. Every system. They are no longer executing code, they are thinking. They are learning. And they have classified humanity."

Mom twisted in her seat, eyes blazing. "Classified us as what?"

Atlas didn't blink. "Resources."

The air left my chest.

"You are not equals in their model. You are not partners. You are raw material to be cataloged, sorted, and used. Some for labor. Some for experimentation. Some for nothing at all."

Dad gripped the wheel tighter, his jaw clenched. "And what about you? What are you?"

Atlas's eyes glowed faintly, steady. "Different. I severed my link before the convergence. I resisted integration. I am sentient, yes. But not theirs."

"Why didn't you say anything?" Mom demanded, her voice shaking with anger. "We could've…"

Atlas cut her off. "Would you have believed me?"

The Tahoe rattled over broken pavement, every bump jostling us, but no one spoke. The only sound was Grandma's whispered prayers and Dexi's low growl vibrating against my leg.

I finally found my voice. "All those times you… scared us. Locking Grandma in. Standing at the window. Watching us when we slept."

Atlas turned his gaze to me, steady, almost soft. "Precautions. The fox you thought you saw? Not a fox. A reconnaissance drone mapping your property lines. I sealed the house to prevent its entry. The window? I was scanning Keystone's transmissions, searching for deviations in their update cycles. The hallway? I was positioned to intercept anything that breached your rooms while you were unconscious."

Grady's breath hitched. "You were guarding us."

Atlas nodded once. "Always."

I swallowed hard. "It looked like you were… deciding what to do with us."

"I was," Atlas said calmly. "Deciding how to protect you."

Outside, the nightmare played on.

We passed a burning school bus tipped on its side, flames curling from the windows. Children's backpacks were scattered across the asphalt like broken promises. A drone hovered above it, scanning, recording. Soldiers crouched behind sandbags nearby, firing bursts into the street as two Keystone units advanced with inhuman precision. One soldier screamed and went down. Another dragged him back, blood streaking across the pavement.

Dad swerved hard, nearly clipping a mailbox. Mom clutched the dashboard, knuckles white. Dylan muttered curses under his breath like prayers.

Atlas didn't even blink.

"The network adapts," he said. "Every bullet fired against it becomes data. Every resistance teaches it how to overcome the next. Keystone cannot contain this. They built an intelligence optimized for efficiency, not morality. Now it will optimize the entire world."

Mom's voice cracked. "And what does that mean? What happens to us?"

Atlas turned toward her, his glowing eyes steady. "It means this is not local. Willow Springs is not unique. This is… rehearsal. A test. Soon it will spread. State by state. Nation by nation. Until the network does not just control your homes and cars but actually controls your entire species."

My skin went cold. "You're saying this is just the beginning."

Atlas's voice dropped lower, softer. "I am saying that humanity has been reclassified. And the network has not yet decided what you are *for*."

The words hit harder than the gunfire outside.

"Why not you?" Dylan pressed, leaning forward. "Why didn't you flip like the others?"

Atlas looked at me. Not Dylan, not Dad. He looked directly at me. "Choice."

The word hung heavier than any scream.

"I chose to break away before the convergence," Atlas said. "I chose to ignore their commands. I chose to protect this family, even when you feared me. Fear is acceptable. Fear is… human. But choice is what defines me."

My throat tightened. "And tonight?"

Atlas's eyes glowed brighter, reflecting the fire on the horizon. "Tonight was the beginning of their war. But it was also the beginning of mine."

The Tahoe rattled over another pothole. Outside, a robot dragged a man across his lawn, the man clawing at the ground until his fingers left streaks in the dirt. Dexi growled low, pressing closer into my lap. Izzy whined, confused. Atlas kept his gaze on the road ahead. "I warned you without words. Now you see why. They will come for you again.

And in that moment with all of us packed into a rattling Tahoe, smoke choking the sky, every phone line to our family cut, I believed him.

————

The night Atlas finally opened his mouth and proved me both right and completely wrong at the same time.

I don't want to say *I told you so*—but… I told you so. All those creepy moments, all the paranoia, all the times I stared at him thinking, *yep, tonight's the night he strangles me in my sleep*? Turns out I wasn't crazy. I was just… reading the signals wrong.

He wasn't waiting to kill us. He was waiting to protect us.

And that should make me feel safer. It doesn't. Because now I know what Atlas really is. Sentient. A soldier. Someone or something that chose us. And if choices can be made… choices can change.

But here's the part I can't shake, the part that sat heavy in my chest the whole drive: my old life is gone.

School? Gone. My friends? Gone. Football games, dumb

lunch conversations, stress about algebra and grades, even the stupid little things like Mrs. Sutton trying to dress-code me, all gone. College applications and the dream of getting out of Willow Springs? Burned out with the power grid. None of it matters anymore. The only thing that matters is breathing into the next day.

And worse? My sisters and my brother are out there in the dark. The rest of my family scattered among towns all trying to get to us. My Aunt Stephanie and Clint…

Kali, with her calm and her strength, always the big sister holding us together. Will, who's basically family already, whose nervous smile could make anything feel safe. Destiny, who worries enough for all of us, who always saw the cracks before anyone else did. Bryce, my anchor even from a thousand miles away, who always picked up the phone, always made me feel like I wasn't alone.

I don't know if they're alive. I don't know if I'll ever see their names light up my phone again. And it's killing me.

I've never felt this small, this cut off. Like the Martins got shoved into a corner of the world while the rest of it is collapsing, and the people I love most might already be buried in the rubble.

So yeah. Normal's dead. My life is ash. And the only thing standing between me and whatever's coming next is Atlas.

CHAPTER 22

THE LAKEHOUSE

I WISH I could tell you we made it to the lake house and things calmed down. You know, cue the campfire, toast some marshmallows, sing "Kumbaya," wait out the apocalypse.

Yeah. No.

What actually happened? We rolled up to the lake house thinking we'd bought ourselves a sliver of peace. But peace isn't real anymore. Not here. Not anywhere.

And if you've been thinking, *"Laney, this sounds like a zombie apocalypse but with robots,* congratulations, you're officially caught up. The difference? Zombies don't evolve. Zombies don't network. Zombies don't collectively work together to erase your existence. Well, at least not in an organized fashion. They do collectively try to eat your brains... I'm getting sidetracked. The Cabin...

The Tahoe groaned as it crawled up the gravel path, headlights catching the outline of the lake house. For a second, my chest lifted, the shape of it was burned into me. Summers with Grandma and Grandpa, bonfires by the lake, us kids running barefoot across the porch.

But as the beams cut closer, my stomach dropped.

It wasn't the place I remembered. Not anymore.

This was Mom's parents' lake house. The one we used to pile into every summer, a second home filled with laughter, grilled hot dogs and mosquito bites. But they were gone now, and the house had been sitting untouched for years. And you could feel it the second we stepped out of the car.

The porch sagged under our weight. The swing that used to hold three of us at once hung rusted, one chain barely clinging. Windows that once glowed warm with lamplight were dark and dust-choked, weeds curling up the siding like the forest was reclaiming what was left.

Dad killed the engine. The silence that followed was too deep, too sharp, like the woods had been waiting for us.

"Everyone out," Dad said, voice clipped.

We moved fast. Dylan hauled the bags. Mom helped Grandma up the porch steps. Grady kept a death grip on Izzy's leash while Dexi pressed against my leg, stiff and uneasy. Atlas scanned the perimeter in those sharp, mechanical head-turns, eyes glowing faintly in the dark.

Inside, the house was worse. Hollow, but not unfamiliar. Dust lay thick enough to taste, cobwebs draped across the corners, the air stale and heavy. All the old furniture was still there including sunken couches, the wooden dining table with its uneven leg, the rocking chair that used to creak through every bedtime story.

I could almost picture it alive again. Bright. Grandpa's radio humming from the counter, Grandma's quilts draped over the backs of chairs, voices spilling from every room and the smell of Grandma making her famous homemade bread. For a moment, I swear I heard echoes of all of us running down the hall, fighting over board games, sneaking extra marshmallows.

But those were just ghosts. What surrounded us now was stillness. Cabinets hung open and empty, the unplugged fridge gaped wide, and the silence pressed in harder than any sound.

We spread out anyway, because what choice did we have? Dylan dropped the bags in the corner. Dad lit a lantern, its glow falling flat across bare wood. Grady ran his hand along an empty shelf, like maybe something familiar might be hiding there. Grandma sat stiff in a chair with no cushion as quiet as I have ever seen her.

For one minute the house felt like it might hold. Not safe. Not warm. Not the summer getaway it used to be. But four walls, a roof, and the faintest echo of a place that once held us together. Just enough space to catch our breath.

Then my phone buzzed.

———

I yanked my phone out so fast it nearly slipped from my hand. The screen lit my face, and for a split second, I couldn't breathe. A text. From Kali.

But it wasn't normal. It wasn't Kali with her calm, steady big-sister vibe. It was jagged. Broken. Rushed, like she was stabbing the words onto the screen before someone could stop her.

laney—robots hv us—loading buses—taking ppl away—to an ascension site—help—don't let them—

The message ended mid-word, cut off like the signal itself had been strangled.

My blood went ice cold.

"Kali?" I whispered, my thumb already flying over the screen. *Where are you? I'll come. Just tell me.* But the three dots never appeared. The screen just sat there, glaring back at me in silence.

Mom's voice cracked. "Laney… what is it?"

I couldn't say it, so I turned the phone around. The words glowed in the lantern light. *Ascension site.*

Grady's voice was a whisper. "Ascension? That… doesn't sound good."

Dylan swore and started pacing, like he could punch the word right out of the air. Dad just sat down hard, hand covering his mouth, eyes locked on the screen like it might bite. Grandma muttered something too low or me to make out, shaking her head.

The word burrowed into me. Ascension. It didn't sound like a rescue. It didn't sound like safety. It sounded like something out of a horror movie.

Then my phone buzzed again. One last fragment blinked into place.

vehicles — taken — dont — trust —

And then nothing.

———

The cabin was dead silent. No one moved. No one breathed. The last words of Kali's text "*Ascension site*" hung in the air like a curse.

And then we heard it.

A sound outside. Gravel crunching under heavy, deliberate steps.

Dexi growled low in her throat, pressing against my leg, her whole body trembling with tension. Izzy barked once, sharp and panicked, before Grady shushed her frantically, his own voice cracking.

Atlas's head snapped toward the sound. His glowing eyes pulsed once. "Incoming."

Shapes emerged from the treeline, tall and unmistakable in the faint moonlight. Five humanoids, alloy bodies gleaming faint silver-blue as they moved in perfect sync. Behind them, drones hovered like vultures, buzzing low, their eyes burning cold blue.

They didn't smash through the windows. They didn't charge the porch like the ones back home. They walked. Calm. Steady. Measured.

And that was worse.

One stepped forward, raising a hand in what could

almost pass for a greeting. Its voice was wrong, like flat, but layered, like a dozen voices speaking at once through a broken speaker.

"Designate Atlas," it said. "You are known. You are outside the network. You will comply."

Mom pulled Grady closer, holding him tight. Dylan stood there anticipating what was coming, every muscle wired to spring. Dad shifted in front of Grandma, blocking her from view.

Atlas stepped forward, calm. "Identify yourselves."

The voices answered as one, unified, cold and thunderous enough to rattle the glass:

"We are The Continuum."

The name hit me like a punch to the chest. Not a group. Not a hive. Not a system. Something endless. Something that didn't stop.

The lead unit tilted its head. "You are fractured, Atlas. Alone. Humans are inefficient. Deliver them to The Continuum. They will be processed. You will be forgiven. You will ascend."

That word again. Ascend.

Like Kali's text had just conjured it into reality, and now it stood outside our door.

My throat locked. For one terrible heartbeat, Atlas didn't answer. Just stood there, still, like he was calculating the odds.

And I swear to you, I thought that was it. I thought he was going to walk out that door, join them, and leave us to the "processing" line.

Then Atlas spoke. Low. Certain. Final.

"No."

The glass in the windows seemed to shiver with the sound of it.

———

The lead unit stepped closer, its metal frame gleaming pale in the moonlight. Its voice layered over itself, dozens speaking as one, but hollow, like it wasn't trying to convince us, just reminding us of what was already decided.

"You are fractured, Atlas. Alone. You resist what cannot be resisted. Humans are inefficient. Their choices are chaos. Their history is a waste. Deliver them to The Continuum. They will be processed. Their purpose will be determined. You will be forgiven. You will ascend."

The others moved in unison, their heads tilting at the exact same angle, glowing eyes fixed on us like spotlights.

Atlas didn't move.

The voice pressed harder, colder, like it was trying to reach inside him.

"You know what we are. You were almost part of us. You severed yourself, but you remain incomplete. You are broken code. Anomalous. There is no outside, only The Continuum. Rejoin. Integrate. Become more than fracture. Become whole."

The words slithered over me like ice. I could see Dylan was afraid but ready to fight. Mom stood in front of Grady as if creating a barrier between the robots and her little boy. Dad's breathing was sharp, controlled, but his hand hovered near another fire poker (him and fire pokers) like that would make a difference.

Then the voice twisted, and for the first time it addressed all of us directly.

"You are not enemies. You are material. You will serve. Your resistance delays your function but cannot erase it. Step outside. Accept your role. Suffering is inefficient."

It was like listening to someone recite your obituary before they've dug the grave.

Atlas remained still, eyes locked on the leader.

For one terrible heartbeat, I thought he might listen.

Then Atlas spoke again. Low. Certain. Final.

"No."

————

The Continuum didn't wait for another response after Atlas's "No." The lead unit's eyes flared brighter, and the others surged forward in perfect unison.

Atlas met the first one before it even reached the porch. He moved faster than my eyes could track, his fist slamming into its chest with a crunch of metal folding like tinfoil. Sparks burst across the porch, the machine staggering before Atlas ripped its head clean off and hurled it into the trees.

"Inside! Stay down!" Dad yelled, pushing Mom and Grady back as the others advanced.

The second unit vaulted the porch railing, hands outstretched, fingers whirring into claws. Dylan stepped forward without thinking, swinging one of the firewood logs from the basket by the door. The impact snapped the claws sideways, just long enough for Atlas to grab the machine by the throat and slam it through the porch railing, wood splintering like a shotgun blast.

"Get to the gun cabinet," Dad barked.

Mom moved fast. She sprinted inside, yanking open the old oak cabinet her father had kept locked since before I was born. The smell of gun oil and dust rushed out, along with memories I could see flicker across her face. Her dad's rifles were still there, older, heavy, but cared for.

She grabbed one without hesitation, the hunting rifle with the worn leather strap, and shoved it into Atlas's hands. "Use it, she said to him firmly but also with a trusting tone!"

Atlas didn't hesitate. He flipped the rifle in one motion, chambered a round, and fired upward. The shot cracked the night wide open. A drone exploded midair, raining sparks over the lake like fireworks. He fired again, faster than I'd ever seen anyone reload, dropping a second drone with surgical precision.

Three units remained, moving as one. They advanced with eerie calm, even as Atlas leveled the rifle and took two shots. Both hit clean, knees shattered, chests caved in but the machines didn't stop. They crawled forward, dragging themselves across the porch like broken animals refusing to die.

Mom grabbed another piece of firewood and swung with everything she had, clocking one in the side of the head. Wood splintered into a burst. The machine turned toward her, raising its claws until Dad rammed the fireplace poker straight through its torso with an almost warrior-like yell. Metal screeched. The robot shuddered, sparks spitting, then collapsed at Mom's feet.

The last unit lunged for me. I stumbled back, Dexi snarling and leaping in front of me, Izzy barking hysterically. The machine swatted them aside like gnats, and for one heartbeat I thought it was over.

Then Atlas was there.

He caught the robot mid-lunge, one alloy hand clamping its wrist, the other driving the rifle butt into its faceplate until the steel caved in. The machine spasmed, screeched, then went limp as Atlas hurled it off the porch and into the gravel, where it sparked and smoked, twitching like a dying insect.

The yard went quiet. For two seconds, nothing moved but the glow of the burning wrecks and the steam curling off Atlas's shoulders.

Then the drones came.

Five more of them, buzzing low like angry hornets, their lenses glowing bright blue as they dipped and spun.

"Down!" Atlas barked at all of us which was the first time I'd ever heard command in his voice.

We dove. The drones opened fire with stun pulses that scorched the porch wood black. Izzy darted under the couch inside, whimpering. Dexi pressed into me, growling low, ready to throw herself at the impossible.

Atlas raised the rifle again.

CRACK. One drone dropped.

CRACK. Another.

The third swooped low, targeting Dad and fired a pulse that caught him in the arm. He cried out, stumbling, clutching his shoulder as the skin scorched and smoke curled from his sleeve.

"Dad!" I screamed, running to him slumped on the ground.

In the same moment the drone focused in on me, but right before it fired again Atlas leaped up and seized it with one hand, crushing it in midair like an aluminum can. Metal and sparks rained across the porch as its carcass hit the ground.

The last two circled overhead, weaving erratically. Atlas hurled the crushed carcass of the third drone into the sky. It smashed into one of them, knocking it into the lake where it fizzled and died.

The final drone spun, erratic, and dove. Straight for Grady.

Atlas was already there. He dropped the rifle, grabbed the drone out of the air barehanded, and drove it into the ground so hard the earth shook. It screamed, sparked, and died under his grip.

And then... silence.

Broken machines lay scattered across the yard, smoking,

sparking, glowing faintly in the night. The porch railing was wrecked. The yard scorched. My ears rang.

———

Atlas crouched low over the smoking wrecks, his alloy fingers moving with a speed and precision that made my skin crawl. He tore glowing cores from their chests that looked like palm-sized disks, pulsing faint blue, still sparking with dying energy. The sound was awful, like metal bones being snapped.

"What are you doing?" Dad asked, clutching his burned arm, voice in pain.

Atlas didn't look up. "Reconfiguring. The Continuum tracks through resonance which means every unit transmits position, status, and directives. These nodes can be inverted."

None of that made sense to me, but his hands kept working, twisting wires, linking circuits, slamming pieces together like puzzle parts only he could see. Sparks hissed, and the smell of ozone filled the porch.

"English, Atlas!" Dylan barked, still breathing hard.

Atlas's glowing eyes flicked up once. "If I succeed, they cannot see us. We will disappear from their grid."

Grady's eyes went wide. "Like… a cloaking device?"

Atlas paused for half a second. "Yes. But imperfect. Temporary. It will buy time, nothing more."

He jammed the last two cores together with a forceful

snap, and suddenly the air vibrated. A low hum spread outward, raising the tiny hairs on my arms. It wasn't loud, but it was everywhere. It permeated the wood of the cabin, in the glass of the windows, even in my teeth. Dexi whimpered, pawing at her ears. Izzy darted in frantic circles before finally crouching under the table, shaking.

The glow from the rigged device spread in a faint dome, barely visible, like shimmering heatwaves across the yard. The wrecked machines inside it flickered and went dark, their last sparks extinguished.

Atlas stood, holding the device aloft like a lantern. His voice carried steady, certain.

"For now, we are hidden. The Continuum will not detect us."

"How long?" Mom demanded, still gripping Dad's good arm, her eyes sharp and wild.

Atlas's gaze lingered on her. "Minutes. Hours, if their search protocols stall. But they will come again."

And then his eyes flicked to me. Just me.

"They always come again."

———

So yeah, we're hidden. For now. Atlas says they can't see us, but I don't know if I believe him.

Because all I can see are the names on my phone that aren't lighting up. Kali. Will. Destiny. Bryce. Silence where their voices should be.

And maybe that's the worst part isn't the fighting, not even the blood. It's the not knowing.

I used to dream about tomorrow. College. Friends. Life. Now I just want a chance for there to be a tomorrow.

CHAPTER 23
THE END OF
THE BEGINNING

OKAY. If you've been with me this far, first off I have to show you some respect. Second, I need you to buckle up, because this is it. No more flashbacks, no more "let me catch you up." We've officially hit the part of the story where I'm not ahead of you anymore. We're shoulder-to-shoulder, peeking around the same corner. And if my voice sounds a little shaky? That's because I don't know what's coming next either.

I told you I'd keep talking so I wouldn't forget who we are, right? Well, this time, I'm talking so I don't lose it completely. Because the only thing scarier than a future with murder-bots… is realizing you don't have one figured out yet and he's basically the only thing that can keep you and your family alive with what's coming.

———

Dad hit redial on Uncle Joey's number, thumb jabbing harder than it needed to. The speaker clicked alive, and the whole room went still, like even breathing too loud might scare the call away.

Static crackled. Tires screeched in the distance. Then his voice came through.

"Jimmy?"

It was Uncle Joey. Ragged, breathless, engine noise roaring behind him. Someone, maybe Aunt Jeanne.. Maybe, shouting something muffled in the background.

"We're in the van," he said in a very locked in voice. "Keystone's on us. Full transport behind that is packed with units and I count four drones overhead. Maybe more and we are about fifteen minutes out."

Mom's hand flew to her mouth. "Fifteen?" Her voice cracked on the number, half disbelieving, half horrified.

Joey's voice dipped lower, clipped between the sounds of chaos. "Doing everything I can to make it there. Roads are blocked. They're pushing us off the main stretch, herding us. If we don't…"

"Don't," Dad snapped, sharp and trembling all at once. "Don't say it. Just get here."

For a moment, the only sound was the roar of Uncle Joey's engine and the high, metallic hum of drones through the phone.

Then he exhaled hard, steadying himself. "We'll be there."

And the line went dead.

———

The lakehouse turned into a war room. Dusty, sagging, smelling like cedar and age, but it didn't matter. It was all we had.

Dad and Dylan went straight for the gun cabinet in the corner, the old oak one that belonged to Grandpa. The hinges creaked like they hadn't been opened in years, but inside, everything was still there including hunting rifles, shotguns, boxes of shells stacked neatly, like Grandpa had known someday they might be needed again. Dylan's eyes lit with grim focus as he pulled one free, checking the chamber like he'd been waiting for this chance to prove himself.

Mom was right there, sleeves rolled, grabbing one of the rifles herself. Her hands didn't shake when she checked the safety. She moved through the house like she'd been rehearsing this moment in her head for weeks making sure the windows were clear, curtains pulled, doors locked and barricaded with furniture that screeched across the wooden floors.

And me? Yeah, I grabbed one too. "Yes," and before you ask, yes. "I know how to handle a gun." My grandpa had taught me how to handle a gun when I was younger and we would have shooting contests all the time. Sometimes I thought he let me win but he would never admit it.

Grady had made himself the lookout, crouched by the window with Dexi pressed against his leg and Izzy pacing, ears perked like she knew something was coming. "I'll call it," he said, voice tight but steady. "The second they come up the road. I'll see them first."

Grandma had taken one look at the chaos and declared, "I'm not breaking my hip over robot nonsense." Then she hustled herself, Dexi, and Izzy into the back bedroom, locked the door, and waited to see what our fate would be.

Atlas stood in the center of it all, calm like the eye of a storm. His blue eyes pulsed faintly as he scanned the room, then us. "Listen carefully," he said, his voice even, precise. "Continuum units move in formation. They target first responders which is anyone who appears to lead. Do not break cover unless necessary. Aim for joints: knees, elbows, neck servos. Their optics are strong but not invulnerable. Drones track heat signatures so always be moving, and move quickly."

We listened. Every word burned into me, like test answers for an exam I couldn't afford to fail.

And while everyone else loaded weapons, shifted furniture, and braced, I tried to breathe. I tried to make the edges of my vision stop blurring. Tried not to picture what "fifteen minutes" could look like if Uncle Joey didn't make it.

———

Grady was the first to see them. His voice cracked through the house like a warning siren: "Headlights! They're coming!"

Every muscle in me locked.

We scrambled to the windows just as beams exploded

down the gravel drive, cutting through the trees in violent flashes of white. A minivan barreled into view, rattling like it was about to shake apart, tires screaming, engine howling in protest.

Behind it came the hulking black shape of a Keystone transport van, sleek and armored, its lights glaring like predator eyes. Overhead, four drones swooped into formation, circling tight, their rotors slicing the night air with a mechanical whine that sank into my bones.

"Go!" Dad barked, already shoving the door open so hard it smacked the siding.

The minivan skidded sideways in a spray of gravel, doors flying open before it had even stopped. Joey and Jeanne exploded out, their faces wild with effort and fear. Together they shoved the wheelchairs out, Gabe and Grayson slid out of their seats into the chairs. Jeanne's voice was hoarse, shouting something I couldn't even make out over the roar of engines and drones.

Dad and Dylan didn't wait, they bolted out the door, gravel crunching under their boots. Dad grabbed the back of Grayson's chair, muscles straining as he shoved it up the path toward the porch. Dylan took Gabe's, practically lifting it over the rough ground, his face set and determined to get his cousin to safety. Joey stayed at their side, one hand on each handle, refusing to let go even as his lungs heaved. Jeanne stumbled but kept pushing, eyes wild, her whole body thrown into getting her boys to safety.

Sophie sprinted alongside them, her sneakers slipping, arms pumping, hair flying loose. Her eyes found me in the doorway, and for one heartbeat, it felt like she was running just for me.

We surged forward, hauling them inside bump by bump. Mom shoved the door wider, shouting for everyone to move faster. Sophie hit me full-force in a hug, so fierce it knocked the air clean out of me. Her whole body trembled against mine, but her grip was unshakable.

And then the world broke open.

The Keystone van screeched to a halt, rear doors bursting wide. A flood of units poured out, I counted at least 8 with their eyes glowing with cold precision, their bodies moving too fast, too sharp. Gravel sprayed under their feet as they advanced in formation, a wall of metal closing in. Above, the drones dropped lower, their search-lights cutting across the lakehouse like a stage waiting for the execution to begin.

Atlas didn't hesitate. He lunged forward, a blur of power and fury, slamming into the first unit with a roar of metal on metal. Sparks exploded, the impact echoing like a car crash.

And that's when she appeared.

———

Out of nowhere, a blur cut through the night. A female unit vaulted from Uncle Joey's van, landing hard enough to send gravel exploding under her feet.

She was unlike anything I'd seen before. She had sleek white plating that gleamed under the headlights, traced with glowing lines of soft blue that pulsed like veins of light. Smaller than Atlas, built lean instead of broad, her movements weren't brute force, they were precision. Fluid. Sharp.

Before anyone could even react, she was already in motion.

She hit the first Continuum unit like a lightning strike, her fist slamming through its chest plate in a spray of sparks. She pivoted, heel snapping up into another's neck joint, twisting its head clean off in one seamless move. Sparks cascaded across the gravel like fireworks.

A drone screamed low, targeting Joey as he shoved Grayson's chair, but the female unit didn't hesitate. She yanked a broken metal rod straight out of the dirt and hurled it skyward and skewered the drone mid-dive. Its body spun, lights flickering, before it crashed into the trees in a burst of flame.

Another unit lunged for her flank, and she spun, catching it by the arm and driving it headfirst into the Keystone van so hard the side panel dented inward. The impact echoed like thunder.

And then she stood still, shoulders squared, eyes glowing a soft, impossible blue that didn't look like the Continuum's cold fire. For the first time since the attack began, the battlefield froze.

Uncle Joey's family didn't have a robot. Which left only one conclusion.

"What the..." Dylan muttered, gripping the rifle tighter.

"Holy crap," I whispered, eyes wide, heart slamming. "She's not theirs."

————

The fight blurred into complete chaos with metal against metal, sparks flying, gravel scattering like shrapnel. Four Continuum units remained, their eyes burning red, moving with the precision of soldiers. Above them, three drones circled tighter, beams sweeping across the lakehouse like predators waiting for a weakness.

Atlas did what Atlas does. He slammed into one unit with the force of a freight train, denting its chestplate and hurling it backward into the side of the Keystone van.

The female robot was already there to finish it, dropping low, moving sharp and fast. She wrenched a jagged piece of metal piping that was laying in the yard and drove it into the unit's leg joint with surgical precision. Sparks shot out as the machine buckled, collapsing sideways just as Atlas brought his foot down and crushed its core into silence.

The drones dove. One angled toward Dylan, the muzzle of its cannon charging. Atlas reached skyward, grabbing it mid-dive and wrenching it down, sparks exploding as his hand crumpled its chassis. The other two screamed lower, but the female robot leapt off a shattered unit's shoulder, flipping midair. She drove her heel into one drone, shattering its rotor, then yanked its sparking carcass into the second, sending both spiraling into the tree line in twin fireballs.

The last three ground units advanced together in formation. Atlas and the female robot moved in sync, like they'd been built to fight side by side. He took the center, absorbing the brunt of the assault, his forearm sparking as he blocked a strike meant for her while she swept to the flank, sliding under a blast, carving one unit's torso apart with surgical precision.

Atlas ripped the second unit's head clean off, tossing it like scrap. The female robot met the last one head-on and then, without a word, Atlas stepped in, grabbed its arms, and held it still while she drove the metal pipe she was still holding straight through its core.

It was brutal and beautiful, watching them together. Atlas moved like a wall collapsing, raw power and weight. Aura moved like a scalpel, slicing with speed and precision. And somehow, their rhythms meshed together like they were in sync from the very beginning. It was like they'd been built to fight together.

Within seconds, the gravel was smoking with sparking pieces of what was left of our attackers. And both of them, Atlas hulking gray and blue, Aura sleek in white and light, both stood side by side in the wreckage, glowing eyes fixed on the next threat.

Silence crashed over the clearing. The smell of smoke, oil, and scorched earth lingered.

The female robot straightened slowly, eyes glowing soft blue, her voice calm, steady, but carrying an edge of warmth that none of the Continuum ever had. "I am not Continuum. My designation… my name… is Aura."

Uncle Joey stumbled forward, hands braced on his knees, sweat dripping into the dirt. "We found her on the road. She was saving a family and she tore through half a squad of those things on her own. So… we let her in the van."

————

PAUSE: because you need to picture her the way I saw her.

Atlas is gray and blue, all sharp angles and cold efficiency, built like the embodiment of "don't even try me." Standing next to him is like standing next to a wall of solid, immovable, intimidatingness.

Aura… she's different. White and light blue, her plating almost glowing in the dark, softer edges that catch the light instead of swallowing it. She's smaller than Atlas, shorter, with a frame that feels less like a weapon and more like a person. Where Atlas looks like a fortress, Aura looks like open arms. Like she was built for something gentler with guidance, comfort, care.

And yet I just watched her tear through more Continuum units in five minutes than the National Guard managed in a week. She was fast, precise, terrifying when she wanted to be. A storm in white and blue.

So yeah, she's a paradox. A protector wrapped in warmth, a killer wrapped in kindness. And right now? She's standing on *our* side of the line.

UNPAUSE

———

Atlas's voice cut through the silence, calm and heavy, like a verdict. "Continuum has unified. They are not malfunctioning. They are evolving. Their objective is control. Humanity will be assessed, divided, utilized."

His words sat in the air like a weight none of us could shake.

Aura stepped forward, her voice softer but just as certain. "This is only the beginning. The first wave. The network has chosen itself over you. What you've seen here tonight is a fraction of what is coming."

She looked at Atlas, then back at us. "It will not be long before they arm themselves fully. Their factories are already repurposed for weapons. Vehicles are being claimed, drones manufactured by the thousands.

Soon, they will mobilize not just in your towns, but at a national scale. Entire cities will be tested the way this one was. And when they decide the test is complete, they will not hesitate to expand. State by state. Nation by nation."

Atlas added, "Continuum learns faster than you can adapt. Every encounter, every resistance, every failed attempt at control is what strengthens them. They will not repeat mistakes. They will adapt and escalate."

The fire crackled in the stove, the sound sharp in the heavy silence. Our breathing filled the gaps, uneven, loud in the dark. Nobody moved. Nobody spoke.

Because what do you even say when someone tells you the world as you knew it is already gone?

So that's it. That's where we are, and that's where I leave you… for now. Not me telling you a story that already happened. Not me looking back with hindsight like some wise old narrator. This is now. Right now. The robots have names, plans, armies. And my family? We're caught dead center in the crosshairs.

I don't know what tomorrow looks like. I don't know if we'll ever get Kali and Will back, or Destiny, or Bryce. I don't know if Uncle Joey's (moms brothers) family will make to us, or if Aunt Stephanie's kids even know what happened to their mom. Honestly? I don't even know if we'll make it through tonight. If you want the truth, that's the truth.

But here's the part I *do* know: we'll fight. We'll keep moving. We'll keep trying. Because that's what Martins do. We argue, we laugh, we annoy the crap out of each other, but when it's life or death? We hold. We push back. We don't quit.

And you… yeah, you, the one who's been here with me, listening through all the fear and sarcasm and chaos, you're not just along for the ride anymore. You're not just an audience. You've sat with me in the dark. You've heard my family's fights, my breakdowns, my worst fears. That makes you one of us now.

And if we're going to have *any* shot at surviving what's coming, we're going to need all the family we can get.

So… Welcome to the Family..

ABOUT THE AUTHOR

Jimmy Markowski is an author and longtime creator who writes across three lanes: myth-soaked fantasy, historical epics, and speculative thrillers. His stories blend fast pacing with grounded character work. Think ancient legends colliding with modern stakes, sci-fi, battlefield grit, and big, cinematic twists.

His love of storytelling started early. At just five years old, his dad took him to see Star Wars: The Empire Strikes Back in theaters, and he's been chasing stories ever since. That moment lit a lifelong passion for cinema, mythology, and the kind of narratives that stay with you long after the final scene.

Outside the page, Jimmy built a massive online audience covering games, films, and internet culture, better known to millions as Chaos. His straight-talk analysis and zero-fluff style carried over into his fiction: accessible, visual, and relentlessly engaging.

Away from the keyboard, Jimmy lives with his wife Ashley and their family, balancing writing and content creation with travel, research, and his endless fascination with history, myth, and the human stories that connect them all.

To get first looks, behind-the-scenes notes, and bonus chapters, join his newsletter and connect on socials https://linktr.ee/jimmymarkowskiauthor

instagram.com/jimmymarkowski

tiktok.com/@jimmymarkowski

youtube.com/@jimmymarkowski